THE
EVOLUTION
OF JANE

The Evolution of Jane

CATHLEEN SCHINE

HOUGHTON MIFFLIN COMPANY
BOSTON   NEW YORK
1998

Library of Congress Cataloging-in-Publication Data

Schine, Cathleen.
The evolution of Jane / Cathleen Schine.
p.   cm.
ISBN 0-395-82657-8
I. Title.
PS3569.C497E9   1998
813'.54— dc21   98-22304   CIP

Book design by Anne Chalmers
Typeface: Linotype-Hell Electra

Printed in the United States of America

QUM 10 9 8 7 6 5 4 3 2 1

To my brother, and friend, Ricky

ACKNOWLEDGMENTS

Darwin ended *The Voyage of the Beagle* by noting that the traveler "will discover how many truly good-natured people there are, with whom he never before had, or ever again will have any further communication, who are yet ready to offer him the most disinterested assistance." To all those members of the American Littoral Society with whom I sailed on the *Galapagos Adventure*, I would like to say, Darwin was right, as always. Thank you for your help and your friendship. And for his generosity in sharing his pleasure in and understanding of the world, I would especially like to thank Mickey "Maxwell" Cohen, teacher, naturalist, guide, and, very simply, the world's best storyteller.

THE
EVOLUTION
OF JANE

THE BARLOW FAMILY TREE

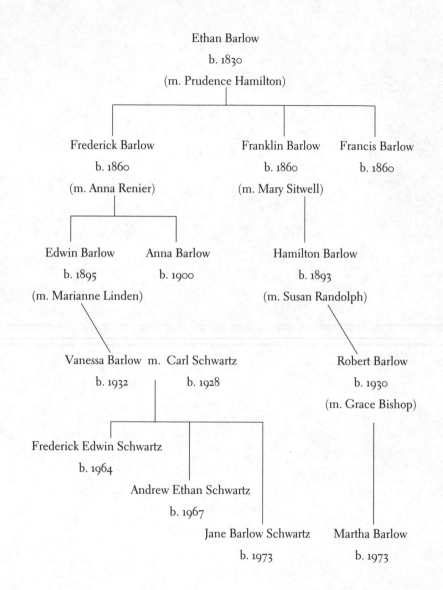

Ethan Barlow
b. 1830
(m. Prudence Hamilton)

Frederick Barlow
b. 1860
(m. Anna Renier)

Franklin Barlow
b. 1860
(m. Mary Sitwell)

Francis Barlow
b. 1860

Edwin Barlow
b. 1895
(m. Marianne Linden)

Anna Barlow
b. 1900

Hamilton Barlow
b. 1893
(m. Susan Randolph)

Vanessa Barlow m. Carl Schwartz
b. 1932   b. 1928

Robert Barlow
b. 1930
(m. Grace Bishop)

Frederick Edwin Schwartz
b. 1964

Andrew Ethan Schwartz
b. 1967

Jane Barlow Schwartz
b. 1973

Martha Barlow
b. 1973

1

~~~mmmmm~~~

HAVE YOU EVER LOST A FRIEND? It is the saddest and
most baffling experience. No one sympathizes, unless the friend
died, which in my case she did not. I lost my best friend many
years ago. She had been my best friend for almost a decade, for
more than half of childhood, and then she evaporated, as though
she had never really existed at all. Did anyone call me, try to console me, try to find a new friend for me? Yet when my husband left
me after six months, I was bathed in sympathy and inappropriate
blind dates. For that brief and absurd episode, I received the most
tender consideration from all around me, most particularly from
my family. Here is the story of my ex-husband: Michael and I were
young and stupid; he, being young and stupid, left me for someone equally young and stupid; I, being stupid, cried for three
months, and then, being young, woke up in the middle of the
night, ate a bowl of cold leftover spaghetti, thought "This is pleasant," and cried no more.

But my mother had become convinced that I needed to "go
abroad" in order to heal, and I did not disabuse her of this quaint

notion. Although I was happier without Michael, I did feel regret at no longer being a wife, if only in an abstract sort of way. Going abroad had such a nice *amour-propre*-restoring ring to it.

"Off you go!" my mother used to say when she pushed me out the door to play, to stop me from moping around the house.

"Off you go!" she said after my divorce. "Off to the Galapagos!"

And so, like many wounded, world-weary souls before me, like Charles Darwin himself, I set sail for the Galapagos Islands. Is a visit to the Galapagos a very odd vacation? It seemed ideal to me the instant my mother suggested the trip. These islands were Darwin's territory, and my mother recalled my childhood infatuation with the bearded nineteenth-century naturalist. She remembered that I wanted to go to the Galapagos Islands when I was a little girl.

In my biography period, I read an illustrated account of the voyage of the H.M.S. *Beagle*, which marked the beginning of my fascination with Charles Darwin. What I remember most vividly from that book was, first, that Darwin was seasick for the entire five years of his voyage on the *Beagle*, and, second, that he had to be very tidy on shipboard. There were pictures of the cabinets used to store specimens, pictures of rows of little bottles and jars and wooden boxes, each labeled in an old-fashioned hand. Life on board ship seemed miniature, like a playhouse full of neatly organized treasures. I'm sure there were pictures in the book of other things as well—birds and volcanoes and ferns—but what I remember most were the boxes and drawers and their orderly tags.

I have had many heroes over the years. But Darwin was one of the earliest. And unlike some of those other early heroes—the Bionic Woman or Pinky Tuscadero, for example—Darwin has aged well. Perhaps because he was so imperfect, because he suffered, because he lived so many lives—a life of physical courage and adventure, a courageous and adventurous life of the mind, a quiet and settled family life. Perhaps because he was such a good gardener. I considered becoming a naturalist, like Darwin. The problem was that once outdoors, I became bored almost immediately. For a while, I persevered, usually by sitting inside thinking I should be a naturalist, sometimes by actually going outside and forcing myself to look at things.

During this time, like all my friends, I also read *The Diary of Anne Frank* and *The Story of My Life* by Helen Keller. But in addition to blindfolding myself and wandering around the living room to see what it was like to be blind the way we all did, and crouching in the attic with a bologna sandwich, hiding from Nazis, I used to look for fossils. I tired of being blind within a few minutes, and I tired of fossils almost as quickly, particularly because I never found any. I did, however, display and label a row of rocks from the driveway. I didn't know what they were and was too lazy to find out, so I just labeled them by color. But I still felt a proprietary bond with Darwin. Whenever I hear his name, to this day, I experience a sudden alertness, as if my own name has been spoken.

When Darwin was a young man, he collected beetles and loved to go shooting. He was supposed to be a doctor like his father, but at the first surgical demonstration in medical school, at the first sight of blood, he fainted. In his subsequent studies for the clergy, he spent most of his time carousing and turning over damp logs looking for insects. It was appealing to me to think that I was making the journey to Darwin's islands much as Darwin had—because the opportunity presented itself and life at home was too confusing. It's true that his parents did not send him to the Galapagos as mine did. In fact, his father was against the idea. But Darwin convinced his family. And so he sailed far, far away on a ninety-foot boat, just like me.

My mother gave me the restorative trip to the Galapagos as a twenty-fifth birthday present. This generous and extravagant gift was from both my parents, actually, but I knew it was my mother's idea. It had the scent of whim, and that's my mother's scent.

"You need to go far away," my mother said.

"Why not the Falkland Islands?" my father said. "That's even farther. And they have sheep."

"Jane is not interested in sheep, are you, Jane?"

"No, not really."

"You see? The Galapagos are perfect. There is not a single sheep."

My mother, a Spanish teacher, found out about this trip through a teachers' organization she belonged to. My father said perhaps she ought to send me to someplace normal, like Paris, for my birthday.

"No," I said. "The Galapagos will be far more consoling."

My father laughed. "I've always found you amusing, Jane," he said, "and so odd."

I hadn't thought much about Darwin or the Galapagos in years, but now, suddenly, as an adult, I wanted to go to those volcanic islands more than I ever had. I was no longer a wife. I had been stripped of my category. So where better to go than to the place where Darwin discovered so many new categories, the place where he discovered the very secret of categories? "I'm not a Coco Island finch anymore," said the little brown bird on the little brown island, "so what am I?" "You're a Darwin's finch," said Darwin. "And you, over there, you're a long-billed finch, and you're a vampire finch"—until all thirteen species of Galapagos finches were detected and named.

What exactly is a species? The definition of a species may seem a simple matter to you, but it puzzled and intrigued me whenever I thought about it, which I must admit was not that often until I prepared to visit Darwin's islands. But once you begin thinking about it, where do you end? I mean, what is it? How do you know? How do you decide? The idea that we all evolved from the same drop of ectoplasmic ooze I have always found to be perfectly reasonable. Nor is it biological diversity itself that alarms me. But look at one mockingbird and look at another. They appear similar, yet they are different species. Look at a Pekingese and a greyhound. They appear different, yet they are the same species.

In my defense, let me point out that the concept of species has changed drastically over the centuries. People have divided up flora and fauna into formal categories since Aristotle—but they keep changing the rules. These days, of course, there are recognized scientific criteria for determining an organism's species. But when I pored over my guidebook looking at pictures of birds and iguanas, I couldn't help wondering who decided what those scientific criteria were and, more important, how they decided. The Galapagos, the islands that had inspired Darwin to find the answers to all my questions, beckoned. I had seen those documentaries of courting blue-footed boobies and giant tortoises chewing cactus. The Galapagos were the frontier of species, and Darwin their pioneer. I was going where Darwin had gone, to see what Darwin had seen.

"You're searching for your roots," my father said, "on a dormant volcano?"

"They're not all dormant."

"Sturdy shoes!" my mother said. "And a hat!"

I had never gone anywhere with a group before, and I tried to tell myself that my Galapagos pilgrimage with the Natural History

Now Society, arranged by my mother, would not be a week on a small boat with an assemblage of strangers, but an enriching apprenticeship. I knew there had to be a reasonable answer to the species question, and I guess I hoped that, traveling with a bunch of nature enthusiasts, I would find it.

———·~~~~///////~~~·———

The trip was in July, and I spent much of the month of June brooding on the nature of species and, in a less abstract but equally challenging vein, shopping. I had to find just the right backpack. I needed the best special quick-drying nylon shorts. There were microfiber shirts and bras and underpants to be acquired, pants that unzipped into shorts and padded moisture-wicking socks, snorkeling booties, gloves and a hood, a wet suit (long or short? how many milligrams thick?), snorkeling skin to wear beneath the wet suit, a Gore-Tex rain jacket, Tevas, summerweight hiking shoes, water bottles, hats, sunglasses, a strap to keep the sunglasses from falling overboard, and of course insect repellent, Dramamine, ginger pills, aloe lotion, and enormous bottles of mighty, waterproof sunscreen. The shopping was satisfying, even more satisfying than shopping normally is, for each purchase was so specialized, made for a reason. A teleological wardrobe. I sometimes think of shopping as a metaphor for life; that is, one tries so hard, picking and choosing, getting as much as one possibly can within one's budget, and then most of it goes in the closet, out of style or too tight in the waist. Then I remind myself that it's the shopping itself that really matters, not the purchases.

"Zen shopping," I once explained to my brother Andrew.

"You have far too much stray information," he said.

———·~~~~///////~~~·———

On July 12, I flew from Kennedy Airport to Guayaquil, a busy, unattractive city on the coast of Ecuador, where I had to change to a smaller plane that could land at Baltra, one of the two Galapagos Islands that has an airport. There, on Baltra, the *Thomas H. Huxley*, chartered by the Natural History Now Society, would be waiting.

On the plane to Guayaquil, I continued to read the guidebook my father had given me, a wonderful natural history of the islands written by a naturalist named Michael H. Jackson. According to Michael H., there are thirteen large Galapagos islands and six small ones, and they "straddle," as he so vividly puts it, the equator at the ninetieth meridian west, six hundred miles west of mainland Ecuador. The Galapagos Islands were first discovered in 1535, first appeared on a map in 1570, and hosted their first resident in 1807—a shipwrecked Irishman named Patrick Watkins. Watkins was stranded for years before he stole the longboat of a passing whaler, enslaved five of its sailors, and rowed away with them. Herman Melville, too, went there on a whaling ship. Melville said that the "chief sound of life here is a hiss." I began to wonder if this vacation was such a good idea after all. Yes, I had seen the PBS documentaries on the soaring albatross, the tortoises, and the boobies with their bright feet. But everyone the guidebook quoted, even Darwin, remarked on how ghastly and glum the islands looked, with burnt fields of ash, jagged black lava, the blinding glare of birdlime.

I was very taken by the book, by the harsh drama of the islands it described, and by the author's name as well. How lucky he was to have a middle name, I thought, under the circumstances. I, too, have a middle name. My middle name is Barlow. Barlow is my mother's family name. It is also the name of the Connecticut town I grew up in, which, as I read about those desert islands I was headed toward, seemed suddenly such an alluring place, so green and inviting.

At the Guayaquil airport, which was small but as lively as a marketplace, I waited to board a midget propeller plane and thought, Why didn't I just go to Barlow?

I was told to line up with the other passengers on the tarmac. With our bags on the ground in front of us, we stood facing uniformed men holding automatic weapons, like prisoners facing the firing squad.

"Terrorists?" asked a woman near me.

"Drugs," said someone else. "Or a coup."

I entertained the idea of a pogrom. I speculated on the possibility of being killed by a death squad before seeing even one species of tortoise. Then a huge police dog appeared, held tight on a thick leash. The military men remained grim as the big dog wagged his tail gaily and pranced along the line of passengers, poking his wet nose at our bags. I wondered if he was searching for a new species.

When the dog was done with us, we finally boarded the plane. An American family of five—grandmother, I assumed, various grown children, and one girl about ten years old, the granddaughter—stood in the aisle, blocking my way, discussing their seating arrangements.

"You can't give Grandpa the window seat," the little girl said with considerable disgust. "He's dead."

"Don't say that," her mother said. "You'll hurt Grandma's feelings."

A guy about my age, the girl's uncle, I supposed, gave me a helpless, apologetic smile. A very engaging apologetic smile. I thought he must surely be with the Natural History Now group, for he was dressed in natural history clothes of khaki nylon and Velcro. But then, so was everyone else. "My guidebook says the view from the left is better," he said. He pointed to an empty seat and I took it. In half an hour I was looking down from the window at a small, dun-colored, flat plateau of volcanic dust surrounded by a flat gray sea.

Charles Darwin visited the Galapagos in the Southern Hemisphere's summer. This is his first impression of the islands: "Nothing could be less inviting than the first appearance. A broken field of black basaltic lava is every where covered by a stunted brushwood, which shows little signs of life. The dry and parched surface, having been heated by the noonday sun, gave the air a close and sultry feeling, like that from a stove: we fancied even the bushes smelt unpleasantly."

I read this passage from the *Journal of the H.M.S. Beagle* on that short flight, and when we climbed down the plane's aluminum stairway onto the runway, I expected to be met by just such a close and sultry feeling, like that from a stove.

I stood at the bottom of the stairway. It wasn't hot at all. It was chilly. I reminded myself that I was there in July, and July was winter in the Southern Hemisphere. Darwin had visited the Galapagos in September, which would have been what? Spring.

Maybe this trip really was a mistake. The sun hung directly overhead. Noon on the equator. I stood beneath the equatorial sun three thousand miles from home, among islands teeming with blue-footed, yellow-scaled, red-throated life, none of it visible, the ground stretching off in cinders. I was traveling with a group of complete strangers. What if they tried to talk to me about the healing powers of crystals? Or Jesus? Or sex addiction? And the islands were ugly—even Darwin said so. And they were cold. These were the islands the Spanish called the Encantadas, the Enchanted Islands. By enchanted, they meant under a spell, they meant cursed.

It was then that I saw a young woman with a sign for our group. I knew it was her. I could tell from across the room. I could tell without seeing her face. There are people you recognize by their general presence. Birdwatchers can identify a bird without really seeing it, by getting just a glimpse, a fleeting movement, the beat of a wing, the flash of a silhouette. The bird flies off, leaving only an impression.

Martha was across the room, obscured by the shade, but I recognized her in just that immediate, intuitive way. I almost expected her to fly off, like a bird, leaving only an impression. Again.

She held a sign that said "Natural History Now." Every group must have a naturalist guide from the Ecuadorian Parks Department. She was our guide.

She was also the girl who had grown up next door to me, my best friend, the one who didn't die, the one for whom I received absolutely no sympathy.

Martha Barlow, my cousin and childhood friend, still my cousin, no longer a child, no longer a friend, standing in the little airport of Isla Baltra, Galapagos, Ecuador, waiting for the group from Natural History Now.

She stared at me.

"You look just like someone I used to know," she said.

"Who?"

"Jane? Is that really you?"

Martha smiled, a pure, involuntary smile that welled up from years and years of friendship. I smiled back. For one moment the simple surprise and fact of recognition hit both of us directly. Then I thought, This is not what I had in mind.

An anonymous vacation with knowledgeable, mildly entertaining, and occasionally enraging strangers was what I'd had in mind. But here was this person who knew me, whom I had once known. Her presence was suddenly not only surprising, but ominous.

"I didn't know you were here," I said.

"I've been down here for a year. I work here. Well, I live here, too. It's so amazing to see you. So weird. Are you actually on this tour? You're in my group! The past rises up and walks upon the earth!"

The friend is dead! Long live the friend!

Martha gave my hand a squeeze. I must admit I was filled with what I can only call joy. Martha, my best friend, among all the strangers and the ashes. But the joy lasted a mere moment. For she was not my best friend, I reminded myself. She had thrown me over, dumped, ditched, cut, cold-shouldered, discarded, shelved, jettisoned, and retired me. I considered asking her right then and there why she'd been so awful so many years ago, so awful that I was reduced to mentally sputtering mixed metaphors. Or not pre-cisely awful, as she had never done anything overtly unkind. She had just stopped being my friend. Stopped, like a clock.

But of course I didn't say, "Hey, you over there, the disloyal, fickle one holding the sign, what the fuck happened anyway?" as I wanted to. For one thing, I didn't have a chance. Martha, the group leader, the guide, was quickly surrounded by her charges. There was a young, heavily equipped couple who introduced themselves as Craig and Cindy Gerrard. Then two women— surely they were at least seventy-five years old—greeted her. One was tall and imposing with a brisk and Tyrolean manner, though she spoke in a thick Queens accent. The other woman sported an alarming amount of aged but still coquettish cleavage. I wondered if Martha worried that these elderly ladies would not be up to the trip. I decided that they both, each in her own way, exhibited quite sufficient vigor. Another aged traveler approached Martha, also a septuagenarian, well groomed, well preserved, small and dapper.

He kissed her hand and said, "And a little child shall lead them!"

Martha greeted the rest—the family I'd seen on the plane, a middle-aged couple, and a woman wearing a United Nations of ethnic garments and carrying an umbrella—and turned back to me now and then to say, "What a coincidence! I can't believe it! "

I had no idea how Martha had come to be a ranger for the Ecuadorian Parks Department. The last I heard was that she was premed in college.

I said, "I thought you were going to medical school."

"I'm a botanist, actually."

"So I guess you never went to medical school."

"Me? No. Did you?"

"*Me?* No. *You* were supposed to go."

"Well, I didn't."

"Well, *I* certainly didn't," I said.

We smiled at each other, both recognizing the comforting, irritable rhythm of a friendship set in its ways. But this intimacy, too, lasted only a moment.

Martha said, "Well!" and resumed her role as guide.

I had successively mourned, demonized, and forgotten Martha, off and on, for quite a few years. Standing in that airport, awkward and uncertain and impatient, I found it hard to believe that now, after so long, Martha could casually greet me, turn easily to the others, nonchalantly turn back again. I don't know what I thought would have been more appropriate. A massive stroke, perhaps.

"We're like your little ducklings," I said. The sound of my voice depressed me. It was forced, lighthearted, one of those voices that have about them a faint echo of desperation.

"Quack," said the oddly dressed woman, and she shook my hand warmly, another member of the flock.

This is where I ought to tell you why Martha and I stopped being friends. The problem is, I don't know. There just came a time when she stopped calling, stopped returning my calls, stopped dead. I never knew what it was I'd done. I just knew that I'd lost my best friend. Or perhaps misplaced her, for here she was again, right in front of me.

We climbed into a launch. The wind blew in our faces. The sea was everywhere. It filled every sense. I tried to think of something to say. Ahead, I could see the *Huxley*, a ninety-foot yacht built especially for ferrying tourists around the Galapagos.

"Our boat is the same size as the *Beagle*," I said.

Martha nodded.

"The *Beagle* carried seventy-four passengers for five years. Can you imagine all those people, all those years on such a small boat?"

"Well," Martha said. "Actually, I forgot to tell you. The trip has been extended! The other sixty people are already on board!"

Our latitude was zero degrees. Martha and I sat in a launch motoring toward a ninety-foot boat at zero degrees. Was that like starting out from zero? Perhaps we could begin all over again, squabbling happily, pretending the last few years had never occurred, ignoring the years of friendship before that. We could meet as if for the first time and proceed from there, from zero degrees latitude. But I saw immediately that Martha was far too familiar to meet for the first time.

The sun was so bright it bleached the sky a pale, pale blue. I put on my sunglasses and watched Martha from behind them. She loved the group already, that was clear. I was sure that she liked all her groups, indulging them, her ducklings waddling all in a row behind her. Martha was not maternal, don't get me wrong. When

she played with dolls as a little girl, they were never her babies—
they were her devoted followers. I was sure that the tourists in every one of her groups were as devoted as her dolls. I always had
been, and old habits die hard: Martha pushed her sunglasses up on
her head, and I felt an awkward urge to do the same.

We climbed a ladder from the *panga*, as Martha called the
launch, to our boat. We were handed up by members of the crew.
All of them then assembled in the main cabin, a lounge with a bar.
There were ten crew members wearing dress-white uniforms, and
as they shook hands and greeted us in smiling, animated Spanish,
I thought that, unfriendly as the islands might be, the *Huxley*, at
least, was going to be an amiable place. The cook, fat and bow-
legged, wore a stiff, sparkling white chef jacket and a tall sparkling
white chef hat that towered officially and absurdly above his white
shorts and sneakers.

We had been ferried to the boat in two *pangas*, and I had gone
with the courtly old gentleman and the two older women, the one
tall and mighty, the other soft, ripe, and risqué, whose names I instantly forgot, as well as the young couple, who both had the soft-
est traces of Canadian accents, and the person of late middle age
in deeply eccentric clothing who had quacked. In the other
panga, there was the middle-aged couple and the guy who had ad-
vised me about seating in the plane along with his family. Although I was rather skeptical about men just at that point, I did
note that he seemed to be single and was good-looking, though
short. And I idly speculated what it would be like to have him as
my roommate on the trip. But I knew the eco-bag-lady was somehow meant for my cabin. There was an unaccountable, hideous
inevitability to it.

I also thought of the possibility of sharing a cabin with Martha,
of course: perhaps forcing the issue of whether we were or were

not still friends by cramped, elbow-jostling intimacy, perhaps to punish her for her disloyalty with constant cold companionship, or perhaps just to have an extended sleepover as in the halcyon days of youth. I wasn't too clear on my motives. But I did realize that Martha probably got to have her own room, like the teacher on a class trip to Washington, D.C. For my hubris in hoping to share a cabin with her, I would be rewarded with the weirdo in the kimono and Ashanti headdress.

I listened almost impassively as Pablo, a very young Ecuadorian with curly black hair and the only crew member who spoke English, gave us our room assignments, and my roommate fears were confirmed.

She waved at me.

I waved back.

Around us rose a confused competitive murmur. Our room was one of only two on an upper deck. Other passengers looked suspiciously at me and the roommate. A silent question rippled through the group: Would our room be better than theirs? Or worse?

It was better. It had windows and a door that opened out onto the deck. The cabins below were prettier, bigger berths, with walls of varnished wood. But they smelled of fuel, and their little portholes were useless. You couldn't open them for air because they were nailed shut, and they were far too cloudy to let in the sunlight. In my cabin, though my knees bumped my roommate's if we both sat on the bunks at the same time, the fresh chill of the air blew through, from door to bright, open window. I was grateful for that breeze, for although we had not yet begun to move, the slight swaying of the boat was already making me a little seasick.

"Just like Charles Darwin himself," said my new roommate, with a reassuring pat on the back.

Our cabin was not much bigger than a train compartment.

Pablo ducked his curly head in the open door to tell us we must each take only one shower a day, or two short showers. Martha had the other cabin on the upper deck. I saw her walk by as Pablo added that we should not flush toilet paper down the toilet, but deposit it in the wastebasket, which he would empty frequently. He spoke in a beautiful, lilting English, which I barely listened to, so intent was I on Martha, incongruous, unexpected, out of place, a fossil, my seashell in the Andes.

My roommate introduced herself as "Gloria Steinham, no relation." I guessed she was about my mother's age, and I suspected that even in that cramped space, her knees would seldom have a chance to bump mine, so infrequently did she sit still long enough to get in the way. She told me she was a science teacher, which perhaps I should have guessed, as she seemed to be wearing around her neck all the specimens she would need for an entire unit on shells, seedpods, or canine teeth. Then she announced that she was never seasick, and that she did not snore.

"Which is a blessing," she said.

"My mother's a teacher, too."

"She should have come with you!"

I tried to picture my mother on the *Huxley*.

"Well, if she could be captain, maybe," I said.

2

~~~~~~~~~~~~~~~~

E<small>ACH MORNING</small>, my mother could be heard saying the same thing: "Chaos." She would murmur it in her soft voice as she mulched her garden or buttoned her coat or stared out the window at a cloudless sky. "Chaos." For years I thought "chaos" was an exclamation of some sort, an expression of abstracted joy, not unlike "wow," for my mother smiled as she said it and shook her head, as if in wonder.

When I think back, her mild observations of chaos were not so much complaints as welcomes, greetings, like a sailor breathing in the salt air. Even her hair looked windblown in anticipation. I used to imagine my mother as a sea captain, like her sea-captain grandfather, Frederick Barlow.

My middle name, as I've said, is Barlow. Jane Barlow Schwartz. My mother did try to use Barlow as my first name, but my father, in this matter at least, prevailed, and I reverted, at age two weeks, to Jane. Of the many ways in which it was unfortunate that my great-aunt Anna, herself a Barlow, chose just that moment to enter senility, the one that affected me exclusively was her conviction, until her death, that my name was Barlow Schwartz, which she repeatedly criticized as silly, undignified, and, worse, unladylike.

"Well," my mother would say to a distressed Aunt Anna, "her name is Jane, but if you insist on calling her Barlow, we could always change it."

"Barlow? Barlow, indeed!" Aunt Anna would say. "Why, you must call me Aunt Anna, of course!"

Sometimes Aunt Anna would introduce herself by saying, "How do you do? I am the skeleton in the family closet." We're the sort of family that has skeletons rather than ghosts, and I'm grateful for that. Ghosts are personal and intrusive, memories that haunt the living. We have neither the imagination nor the patience for ghosts in my family.

Skeletons, on the other hand, are the real thing. Skeletons hold everything together. Skeletons hold the past. They hold information. That's why Darwin collected skeletons. On one of his many inland excursions from the *Beagle*, Darwin visited a place in Patagonia called Port Desire. One of his traveling companions shot an emu, which is some kind of big flightless bird like an ostrich. It was smaller than the other emus he'd seen, so Darwin thought it was an immature member of that species, a young rhea. Only after the little ostrich was cooked and eaten did he realize it was probably a specimen of a smaller, less common species, which he had heard about but had never seen, though he had been searching for one for months. He scraped the bones from the plates, gathered up the remaining bits of feathers and skin and, *voilà!* Ostrich stew transformed into *Rhea darwinii*, a new species stuffed and on exhibit at the Zoological Society.

Skeletons don't come and go like ghosts, even after they've been served for dinner. You can study them, measure them, read the past in them. They're as faithful as dogs. I have tried to examine my friendship with Martha, my former best friend, in this manner. If only I could scrape her off my plate and pick at the bones of our friendship and glue back the feathers.

There's one old shard that I'm particularly attached to—an event that occurred when Martha went on a trip with her parents. She asked me to water the plants she was growing for a science project. I remember the plush emptiness of her house as something thrilling, secret. I walked up the stairs to Martha's room and stood on the threshold looking in with an almost guilty excitement. It was just Martha's room, a canopy bed, a prism hanging by the window, a poster of Madonna. I watered the plants. Then I left Martha a note saying I had been there. I drew a heart and signed it. I felt suddenly self-conscious about the heart. I put a question mark beside it. And I left.

Martha asked me about it when she got home.

"It looks sort of mean," she said. "A heart with a question mark."

"It wasn't meant to be mean," I said.

"Oh. Okay." And that was it. Martha crumpled the note, threw it away, and it was only later, when we stopped being friends, that I thought of the question mark and the heart again. Why did I draw a heart? Because I loved Martha? Why did I write a question mark? Because I was embarrassed about having such strong feelings for Martha? Why did Martha even mention such a stupid, unimportant note? Because it really said so much? Were Martha's feelings hurt? Why would her feelings be hurt by an offhand note? Did my explanation soothe her feelings? Did she, years later, think of that note? Did she think, "Jane is peculiar, both excessive and stingy in her affection. Who needs a friend like that?" Is there anything more petty, more exalted, than a friendship between two girls? How did mine go wrong?

Martha took up almost as much of my energy when we stopped being friends as she did before we stopped being friends. I want you to understand that there were long stretches of my life during which I did not think about Martha Barlow. There were many such stretches, days and weeks and months. I fought with my parents, fell in love with boys, studied for exams, and went to Europe. I graduated from college, got an apartment, got a job, got married, got divorced. My life was full of joy and annoyances, just like the next person's. I didn't sift through Martha's trash in the middle of the night. I was not insane. I was just haunted.

I was haunted by her absence. Did I say, just a moment ago, that my family did not have ghosts? That we had skeletons instead? Skeletons in our closets? Well, I was haunted by Martha, and if that makes her a ghost, so be it. I stand corrected.

Martha first appeared in Barlow when she was eight and I was seven and a half. She and her parents were going to spend the summer in the house to the west of ours. There was another house to the east. Ever since I can remember, and before that, too, those neighboring houses were a source of mortification for my mother. All three houses were identical, three white houses balanced on the cliffs above the sea. They had been built by my great-great-grandfather for his three children, triplets named Frederick (my great-grandfather), Franklin (Martha's great-grandfather), and Francis (he never married, seeming to prefer sailors to women). The three brothers were ships' captains who prospered and caused their New England village to prosper to such an extent that the town fathers rechristened it "Barlow" after its own favorite sons.

By the time my parents got married and moved into the house with my grandmother, the Captain Francis Barlow house to the west had become a clubhouse bordered by a golf course and tennis courts. A gray wooden staircase scaled the cliff from beach to house, and club members in bathing suits traipsed up and down from June till September. We were far enough away not to be disturbed by noise, and gradually my mother came to accept the Barlow Country Club, almost as if she herself had established it, like a Rockefeller letting the commoners walk his Pocantico pastures. But the Captain Franklin Barlow house was a different story.

Just half a mile down the road, beyond the meadow and the stand of trees that bordered our property and signaled the beginning of theirs, stood a house that mirrored ours in every way, and yet no one would have had the slightest difficulty distinguishing between them. For the shutters, which sagged and gapped and faded into their dotage at our house, hung straight and bright on theirs. At our house we believed in crabgrass the way others believe in the stars—crabgrass was less than a religion, but it held meaning. And that meaning was: Look how green and lush a weed can be, look at the pretty yellow dandelions. And all without watering! The lawn spread out from their house in manicured opulence. This house was Martha's. Visiting Martha, I would walk through the field and beneath the trees until I reached that carpet of grass. Then I would ascend the stairs to the large porch, continue across the polished floor, through the open door, where I would stand for a moment, alone and awed by the wallpapers, by the splendor and order and spotless peace, and I would sigh happily, and I would say, "Chaos."

Until the summer I met Martha, the house had looked almost as disreputable as ours. Her parents, who lived in New York City, had rented it out for years and years. I loved the two men who were the last in a long line of tenants. Pan and Sven. They were ballet dancers. They drove a red sports car and were waiting for a check from Sven's father, a famous novelist who lived in Mexico. Pan colored in his bald pate with some kind of brown pencil, and he made this shiny pretend hair come to a point in front, like a cartoon devil. Pan and Sven fascinated me, and I begged to take ballet lessons from them instead of from Madame de Fornier. Unfortunately, they were arrested before I started. They were con men. There was no check, no famous novelist father in Mexico or anywhere else, no roles in the Paris ballet. Just charm and a leased red sports car and a painted point of hair. How I missed them when the police came and took them off in handcuffs. Even then they both looked suave and insouciant, words I learned from them. Sven waved, lifting the policeman's hand with his as he did so. Pan winked and his chiffon scarf blew behind him in the breeze.

"I will miss them, too," my mother said, kissing me on the head. "Though, really, they pruned that lilac to within an inch of its life."

The house stood empty for a while, then I noticed some activity, cars driving into the driveway, people opening and closing the front door. My mother pretended nothing was happening. But something was happening. First, the workmen came. They replaced the old roof with shingles of golden wood. The house, like the others, was large and square, built in 1860. I watched the workmen that summer without wondering who might be moving in. Maybe I thought the workmen were moving in. Probably the next step just never occurred to me. The activity itself was enough. To see the mirror of my own house transformed—first gutted, then put back together like a new breed of Humpty Dumpty—was riveting. I sat at the edge of the trees on the trunk in a weeping willow that had taken a convenient horizontal twist and watched in open-mouthed abstraction.

It wasn't that I was alone before Martha came. I had my two brothers who, though they were so much older than I was, tried to make contact every once in a while, like those people who beam radio messages into outer space, just in case. And there were my parents, of course. My great-aunt Anna did not yet live with us, but even so, there were enough of us so that it never occurred to me I was lonely. It was only when I saw Martha, a little girl, a person who resembled me in height and weight and the pitch of her voice, galloping like a horse across her lawn the way I galloped across mine—it was only then, months after the workmen had come and transformed the house, as the family drove up in a blue station wagon and a little girl my age jumped out and galloped, that I realized I needed a friend.

Martha saw me that day as I sat and watched from the weeping willow tree. She smiled, slowed her imaginary horse to a walk, began to approach me, then suddenly was whisked off by the unruly steed.

"Whoa!" she cried. "Whoaaaa!"

I was tempted to run out and join her. I recognized her invitation. But I just sat and waited in my tree, dumb and agog, until she got bored racing all over her new lawn and ran over as if she had no horse at all, and said, "Look! I have braces!"

She did indeed sport an impressive set of shiny braces, which made me instantly jealous. But as she was a newcomer, almost a guest, I asserted my native superiority and personal liberality by being gracious.

"And a new house," I said.

"No. It's really old."

Martha and I then entered our first of many arguments, pedantic but passionate exchanges, and our friendship began.

"New to you," I said.

"But not to you."

"I already have a house, *just like* this one, and my house is *really, really* old." I was proud of our house, and pride has always confused my debating abilities.

"See?" she said.

"A *hundred* years old."

———

I walked home through the meadow that day in a thoughtful frame of mind. It was August and the Queen Anne's lace was as high as my chin. The sticky milkweed was even higher. The bees were out. Their noise was close, but muffled by the tall weeds. Above, the sky was so blue I wished the jungle of stalks around me would part and let me see it fully, an endless bowl of sky. Or that I was taller and could stroll through the wildflowers and skunk cabbage without noticing them, the way my father did, and my brothers, and my mother, all of them wading through the field without a thought, the jungle no jungle at all to them, the sky theirs for the looking. I glimpsed patches of blue, breathed in the damp, flowery air, smiled a secret smile hidden by green, and allowed myself to feel the thrill of new, sudden intimacy.

Much of the facade of our house was adorned by lilac bushes, and between their gray stems, as thick as little trunks, and the weathered white paint of the house, were several indentations in the packed dirt where the dog went to rest when the sun was high, and where I often joined him. I crawled past the porch's edge to the first dip in the ground, and there he was, silently thumping his tail. I suddenly knew I would spend less time crouched beside him in our hiding place and I felt disloyal and sad and, at the same time, as happy as if I'd fallen in love, which, of course, I had.

"Good-bye," I said, formally, politely.

When I got inside, into the soft, caressing gloom of our house on a sunny day, I passed my father in the hall and told him about the little girl in the house next door.

"Uh-oh," he said. Then he laughed and offered me a puff of his pipe, a little joke between us which annoyed my mother, who seemed to think, each and every time, that I would actually take him up on it.

I pushed past him, and said, "Not just now, thank you. I'd prefer a cigar," which is what I always said, though this time I was impatient to be off to my mother. "Cuban."

Perhaps this is the place to tell you that my mother, my mother the Barlow of Barlow, is actually, like those imaginary cigars we used to torture her with, Cuban herself. She was born there, anyway, and lived there until she went to Vassar. My father is a Schwartz of Brooklyn. I was never sure why they lived in Barlow because both of them spoke with such tender nostalgia of their former residences, and yet I could not imagine them anywhere but Barlow.

"We are the closest extant Barlows they've got," my mother said.

"You know, they really ought to rename the town Schwartz," my father said.

Then Martha's Barlows came. But Martha's family, according to my mother, were interlopers.

"We are endemic," she said. "They are introduced."

On the day I met Martha, I went looking for my mother and I found her in the garden. She tended her garden with maternal care. Seeds were tucked gently into little cardboard cups before the snow melted. The ground was combed and nourished in spring, blanketed with pine needles in winter. In return for her care, the garden gave her roses and, more important, lilacs. Every kind of lilac grew around our house, deep purple, pale violet, white, even the rare yellow lilac. My mother ordered plants from nurseries sometimes, but often she just scoured the gardens of the neighboring towns, surreptitiously taking cuttings when she found some variety that was really worthwhile ("You simply *can't* buy this," she would say, triumphant, holding the purloined bloom in her arms like a baby).

My mother sometimes said that the only reason she stayed north was the lilac, that you couldn't grow lilacs in Cuba, though you could grow anything else and everything else, things to eat, papayas dropping of their own free will into your open hands, golden bananas lining the streets.

The lilacs bloomed only in spring, for a few short weeks, which made them even more precious. For the rest of the growing season, my mother contented herself with roses. I watched her now as she stooped among them, then stood up to face me, a narrow figure in jeans and an old blue shirt of my father's: a pole of blue reaching up to the straw hat from which an enormous circle of shade spread around her. I often thought my mother looked like a tree. Today, the tree she looked like was a palm tree. And from up there, in her highest branches, she spoke.

"Jane, do you have to pee, honey?"

Horrified, I put my hands on my hips and scowled. I know when I scowl because my whole face stretches down in a most satisfying way. And by the age of seven, my scowl was already quite accomplished. I had been practicing in the mirror for years.

"You're squirming," my mother said.

"There's a new girl," I said. "At the new house."

"It's not new," my mother said, and turned back to her roses without another word.

I tried again to get her interested at dinner that night, but she ignored me, smiling and saying something in Spanish to my father.

"I don't speak Spanish," he said.

"And it *is* new," I said. "To *them*."

My brothers gave each other looks at the sound of the word *them*, looks that meant they knew something interesting to which I was not, and was not going to become, privy.

"What?" I said.

"Nothing," said my father.

Sometimes in these situations I had to wait a long time until someone cracked or accidentally let a word drop or spoke thinking I was in bed when I was sitting on the stairs, my knees up to my chin beneath my nightgown. It took almost a month to learn about Cousin Edna's abortion, and almost a year after that to discover what an abortion was. But often all I required was a minute or two, a caesura of calm. My family's attention usually wandered away from me very easily, in truth. So I waited at the table, quiet and inconspicuous.

"You shouldn't speak Spanish to me, my dear."

"Oh, pooh. Why not?"

"*Parce que le pickup ne marche pas*," said my brother Andrew. He was thirteen and had just started French in school.

My mother shrugged. She drank some wine. A whole glass of wine. I was more and more hopeful. With even one glass of wine, her cheeks would turn pink, as pink as one of my mother's Bourbon Queen roses. She rarely had two, for she might become sleepy and dreamy. But with this one glass, I thought she might at least get flushed and cheerful and talkative. I looked at Fred, my oldest brother. He was going to college next year and I would miss him. I thought Fred was extraordinarily handsome and had always wished that I looked like him. When he developed a twitch a few years before, I was so impressed that I began to twitch, too, in imitation, and had been sent home from school by a worried nurse. It seemed so urbanely adult that I refused to stop blinking until he stopped, which luckily he did after only a week or two.

"Let's forget it," Fred said. "All of it."

"Fine with me," my father said. "It's not my family."

That was all I got that night, though I sat motionless and silent, as patient as a post. It wasn't until the next morning that I understood that the family that was not Daddy's family was Mommy's family. I saw their new mailbox, which had the number 27 on it. That had always held some interest for me, for ours was number 17 and between our two houses there was only the meadow and the line of trees. Why had the town numbered ten nonexistent houses? There was a subdivision across the street full of split-levels, but it had its own road, Jennifer Circle, named after the builder's odious daughter Jennifer, who told everyone that my house was haunted. I suppose the town had numbered the houses in that way because it foresaw the land being sold off to developers someday and wanted to save everyone the trouble of fractions on their mailboxes. I would sit on the side of the road and pretend I was looking at the ten phantom houses, looking in their windows, at the cars in their driveways. Number 18, number 19, number 20—who would live there? Number 21, 22, 23, 24. Would they have children? 25, 26. Would they have a dog? On hot days when I was too enervated to do anything but sit by the road and pout and throw stones, I would populate the entire area with imaginary friends and foes. But now here was a real family in number 27, and on their mailbox in black letters was the name "Barlow."

At first I thought Barlow referred to the name of our road. I waited at the mailbox, sitting in the gravel on the side of the road and drawing designs in the sand with a stick. I knew the girl I'd met yesterday would see me, and I knew she would come out when she saw me. I imagined what a tempting sight I was to a new girl in the neighborhood, one who had not yet made any friends. At least I would have been a tempting sight to myself, a girl squatting in the dirt, doodling. And indeed the new girl soon materialized, squatted beside me, and began her own design. We neither of us spoke at first. She may have felt shy, but I was simply happy. The sticks scratched in the sand, scraping a soft message, a code of random swirls that both of us understood perfectly. We could have been drawing up legal papers, signing a declaration, writing a poem.

"I'm in third grade," said the girl.

I was about to say, "Me too," but then she added, "Going into fourth."

"Oh."

She stopped drawing and pointed the stick at me.

"I'm going into third," I said.

"I know," she said. "Your name is Jane. You're my cousin."

"I am?"

"Yeah. But let's be friends."

I don't remember what I said to this proposition. Probably I just stared with my mouth open.

"I'm not really going into fourth grade," she added.

Her name was Martha, she said, Martha Barlow. See the mailbox? It says "Barlow" right there. Just like the name of the street. I noticed that she called our road a street. I remember that it sounded so urban. We were distant cousins, she said. Her great-grandfather used to live at 27 Barlow Street. Her parents had decided to fix up the old house, to rescue it to use as a summer house. I remember that too, that they had come to the country to rescue the house, as if Barlow were the country and not a town, as if one couldn't live there in the winter, as if their house needed to be rescued.

"They came to the country to rescue the house," I said to my mother that afternoon. "For the summer."

"Oh, please."

"You didn't tell me we're cousins."

My mother didn't answer me, but she pulled me over to her and gave me a hug. She kissed the top of my head. In this way she communicated to me that while Martha was very much at fault for being my cousin, I was in no way to blame for it myself. My mother was an amazing combination of the critical and the accepting. She shimmered back and forth, like a color you can't quite name. Is it teal or slate or gray, or threadbare black?

I asked my father that night what was going on. My father had big ears. I mention this because his ears were very dear to me as a child. They were comforting. My father was not the gentlest person of my acquaintance. He was compact and muscular, he spoke in a growl. Most children were afraid of him. I knew him, so of course I wasn't afraid one bit, but when he seemed particularly gruff, I would look at his ears, and I would be reassured. I found my father sitting on the porch, having a drink. His tie was off, draped with his jacket over the railing, and his white shirt was damp and wrinkled. Unlike most of the fathers I knew, mine always wore penny loafers, buffed to an impossible shine, though they were so old that they were as wrinkled as a face. I loved his shoes and I looked at them tenderly, looked at his nice, big ears and, ignoring the tinkling ice of his drink, the sound of an adult relaxing, an adult who wanted to be left alone, I climbed onto his lap.

He kissed me and offered me his drink, even though my mother was nowhere to be seen and so could not benefit from this provocation. My father always offered me coffee or Scotch or a puff on his pipe. My mother knew it was a joke and knew I never accepted, but she couldn't help herself and she would glare at him, and say, "Carl!" in her most severe voice. Then my father and I would laugh the laugh of collusion.

"Oh, Daddy," I said, pushing the drink away.

He shrugged.

"Daddy?"

"Mmm?"

"Daddy?" I said again. I knew this was a mistake. I knew he would now sigh in that weary parental way. I knew I should just say what I had to say. "Daddy?"

He sighed the sigh I had been expecting, the sigh I hated, for it made the distance between a child, that is, myself, and an adult, that is, all the important people in my life up to that point, so manifest.

Helplessly I again said, "Daddy?"

He said, "What, Jane, what?"

Then I told him that the Barlows were our cousins. "Why is that such a big secret? Mom is very strange."

"Your mother is very strange, but it can't be a very big secret if you know it, can it?"

"It's not a secret," my mother said, coming out onto the porch. "It's a blight."

"Well, let's say they have a past, okay?" my father said.

But everyone had a past. Even I had a past. I could remember my grandma Barlow, a tall bosomy person who took me on her lap to tell me stories of Cuba and tales from the Bible, which left me certain that Havana was on the Red Sea, that manna and mangoes were closely related, that the Burning Bush gave off a scent of vanilla. I had a past, though I was not yet eight, and my past opened on to the pasts of others. I must have looked as confused and disgruntled as I felt because my mother burst out laughing, and said, "Poor-r-r Hayne," in an exaggerated, comic Spanish accent, and my father began to try to explain the Barlow past to me.

"It was so long ago," he said, "that it won't matter to you. But sometimes families have . . ." He paused.

"Wars," my mother said.

"Yes, all right. Civil wars." He told me there were three Barlow brothers, which I already knew, and so I grew impatient and stopped listening for a while. When I tuned in again, the relatives swarmed like flies. Frederick, Franklin, and Francis. Francis died a bachelor without issue. Franklin had one son named Hamilton and was Martha's great-grandfather. Frederick had two children, one of whom was my grandfather Edwin, the other my great-aunt Anna.

But never mind about Aunt Anna now, my father said.

"I shall always mind about Aunt Anna," my mother replied. I thought her tone rather dramatic.

"I don't mind Aunt Anna," I said. "I like Aunt Anna." She was a jazzy old thing, literally banging out tunes of the Roaring Twenties on her piano.

"Well, why wouldn't you?" my mother said. "Do you want to visit her tomorrow, Jane? I'll take you with me."

Visiting Aunt Anna was a great treat. She still lived alone in a narrow brownstone in New York City, and she pinned notes to all the furniture telling her where she was and what she had to do. They said things like:

> REMINDER:
> 1. *Sort photos.*
> 2. *Cocktails.*

It was always possible the note was recent, but Aunt Anna could just as easily have pinned it there five years earlier. At any rate, she would say, "Cocktails!" and clap her hands in anticipation, then dutifully begin sorting photographs in preparation.

"Gone west," she would say every once in a while, shaking her head, looking down at a picture of a sepia face in a high collar or a figure in a creased black-and-white snapshot.

Aunt Anna had a large, unpleasant black Persian cat, and would invariably say, "I have a soft, lovely black pussy," much to my brothers' amusement. And she had portraits of two of the triplets — Frederick, her father, and her uncle Francis.

I always felt a particular bond with Francis. Once, standing beneath this painting of him in his stiff black suit, I asked my mother to define the word *ironic*. I used to plague my mother with this question. Nothing had satisfied me up to that point. Every explanation or example seemed to me to describe something that could just as easily be called sarcastic or coincidental. The nuance of the word escaped me, and bothered me in some deep, philosophical way, until Great-Uncle Francis was invoked.

"So, what does it *mean*?" I asked yet again.

"Aha!" Aunt Anna cried out from another room. "Francis Barlow, captain of a fleet of merchant ships, died at sea."

I assumed at first that this was one of Aunt Anna's quaintly senile non sequiturs. But then she appeared in the doorway, looked at Great-Uncle Francis on the wall, and said, *"In a pleasure yacht,"* and I understood.

Aunt Anna had a housekeeper, too, almost as old and dotty as she was, who came in every morning at eight and left every evening, after cocktails with my aunt, precisely at eight, though how she told the time I don't know, for every clock in the house was set to a different hour. Some of them chimed and, because they all struck the hour at different times, there was a great deal of soft musical clanging at Aunt Anna's.

"You love to go to Aunt Anna's, don't you?" my mother said.

"And I can bring Cousin Martha!" I said.

"No," she said.

"But they're related."

"The sins of the father," said my brother Fred, walking past us and up the stairs.

"Daddy has no sins," I said. "Do you?"

But my father did not answer, for he had already resumed droning on about people I had never heard of, never met, some of whom had sold part of the company and kept the money, which was why my grandfather had to go to Cuba.

"Is that why they can paint their house and get a new roof and pave the driveway and we can't?" I asked.

My father laughed.

My mother said paving the driveway was vulgar.

3

~~~~~~

MARTHA ANNOUNCED on that very first afternoon in the Galapagos Islands that we would take our first Galapagos field trip to a beach called Las Bachas. I would tread in Darwin's footsteps! Never mind that he had not gone to the island where Las Bachas was. Darwin visited only four of the islands, where he spent a total of only three weeks. But the Galapagos were his, and now they were going to be mine as well. I was so keyed up, so intoxicated with Darwin and his islands, and at the same time so agitated by Martha, that I don't think I really distinguished between the two. Martha was to lead me in Darwin's footsteps. Or Darwin in hers.

We unpacked and then lined up like children to go down the gangplank, if that's what you really call it, to the little open motorboat. The *panga* would then ferry us, in two trips, to the island, which was just across a tiny bay from Baltra. I was in the second group, and while we waited for the *panga* to return, enormous black frigate birds coasted across the sky and we saw a baby hammerhead shark swim by.

The fresh, salty perfume of the air was exhilarating. The sun was bright and was above us, the sea was green and was below us. But I was disoriented in a profound way. I had no idea where north was no matter how many times Ethel, the tower of seventy-year-old health, pointed it out to me. I had no landmarks. The sea and the sun were an eccentric sea and sun.

We climbed down into the *panga* and skimmed across the Pacific Ocean to a low, dark shore. We climbed out of the *panga* into icy knee-deep water. I thought, I'm straddling the equator. Martha stood in the water and helped each of us out of the launch. I was last.

"There, now," she said.

I glanced at her to see if this utterance was deliberate. We had often embarked on prolonged discussions of "there, now" as children, an exclamation I had deemed redundant and, worse, senseless.

"What does it *mean*?" I would say.

"It means 'there, now'" was all that Martha would reply.

I checked once more, hoping to catch some flicker of a smile, some knowing look back at me, but she was already scanning the skies with her binoculars.

"Audubon shearwaters," Martha said. She pointed to a flock of dark, diving birds.

The beach curved in a tight crescent, a white flash in the black rock. The rocks, so dark, were ornamented with dozens of large and very red crabs.

Martha lowered her binoculars, and we walked silently along the wet sand toward the others.

The island itself was so unreal, so singular. It seemed all the more bizarre with Martha walking upon it.

"So," I said. I was startled by the Galapagos. There was something extreme about this little island with its glaring white beach and glaring black rocks and glaring red crabs. And I continued to be startled by Martha.

"So!" I said again. And then, "You're the guide."

I had traveled across two continents, from one ocean to another, in order to be washed up on a beach with my next-door neighbor. And she, who as a girl could not see the ineffectual nature of the phrase "there, now," did not seem to be able, as an adult, to recognize the magnitude of the miracle of our Galapagos reunion.

"Here we are in the Galapagos," I said. "Where the greatest revolution in modern thought was born."

I looked around, trying to take in the vastness of the island's isolation, which gave the place a feeling of being both very big and very small at the same time.

"Greater than Marx's, " I said.

Yes, but—all that childhood sincerity, all that competitive worship, all that sarcasm, all those secrets and confessions and fashion tips—all, all for naught. Friendship betrayed, played false, delegitimized like a tyrant state, a banana republic.

"Greater than Freud's," I said.

Martha pointed out some brown noddies. The shearwaters dove into the waves rolling toward the beach, then emerged, swallowing their catch. Fish gotta swim and birds gotta fly, but what is the purpose of friendship? It seemed to me at that moment that friendship could be nothing more than a mistake, a mutation, a freak, a *lusus naturae*, a joke of nature—what Darwin called a sport.

"I was so surprised," Martha said. "I couldn't believe it when I saw you. I'm so glad you're here."

Well, not a *mutation*, I thought. Not quite that. What a desperate, irresolute organism is human consciousness. At least my consciousness was, wagging its tail, leaping for joy: its master's voice!

"Why *are* you here?" she added. She said it in a kindly way, and, after all, why *was* I there? But the question established turf so clearly. She might just as well have pissed on a tree. Human consciousness put its tail between its legs.

"My mother sent me."

"You're lucky," said my roommate, Gloria, coming up on my other side. "My mother sent me to boarding school."

"Why are *you* here?" I asked Martha.

"Oh, too existential," said Gloria. "Why is any of us here? In this great wide world? Our mothers sent all of us! Some of us had to go to Rosemary Hall, too, that's all."

She veered off to photograph some indistinguishable birds flying in the distance.

"What have you been doing all these years?" Martha said.

I told her I worked at the Culture Foundation, a weekly gathering of academics as well as various institutionally unaffiliated pillars of the intellectual and artistic community.

"Or rather," I said, adopting my best witty New Yorker attitude, "since there is no real intellectual and artistic community in New York anymore, and since the Culture Foundation was begun in order to encourage the growth of just such an intellectual and artistic community, I think of the Culture Foundation as more of an artificial body, like a Frankenstein's monster. Random, ill-fitting parts which all get together in one room once a week."

I paused to see if she had been impressed by my eloquence.

"So what do you do there?" she said.

"The mailings, the schedule of talks. Sometimes I type up their talks for them or their notes. Anything anyone wants me to do, really. They also come to be fed during these weekly gatherings, which are therefore called Lunches. I call them, send them invitations, remind them, find them chairs, greet their guests, order the sandwiches and salads. And I listen. That's the best part. It's like school without grades. If it weren't for the unfortunate salary, it would be a perfect job."

"A sort of free-floating apprentice," she said. "Just what you always wanted to be."

It was true. When I was a child, I wanted to grow up to be an apprentice. It didn't matter what kind of an apprentice. It was the idea of apprenticeship, or perhaps just the word itself, that appealed to me. And now I was an apprentice with no field, no territory, no turf, no master, even. I loved my job, for it allowed me to rub shoulders with ideas, to listen without having to retain, to gather information like flowers.

"Yes. My apprenticeship is very pure," I said.

Martha was silent awhile, then said, "It's such a great group."

"A bit vainglorious," I said, "but not too demanding about their grub. As long as there's enough." Then I realized she meant us, the Galapagos ducklings. *Her* group.

How does one define a group? Kingdom, class, family, genus, species. Did I leave any out? Phylum? It had occurred to me only the night before, in the five minutes before I fell asleep, that genus is generic and species is specific.

Which group was this line of tourists on a beach? And how could Martha stand it, another batch in gray suede hiking boots and floppy hats replacing the last identical batch? Telling strangers the same thing over and over, learning all their names, forgetting all their names, learning the next group's names, on and on, leading an endless parade of well-meaning nature lovers seduced by public television documentaries. She walked among us, an oddly urban figure, wiry and remorseless, as if she were looking for a cab in the rain.

"And what, I wonder, is the story behind this little number?" the dapper elderly man asked Martha. He pointed to a stringy vine crawling across the sand. He tilted his head in an insinuating way.

"He's a retired gossip columnist," Gloria whispered to me. "Jeremy Toll. Remember? 'Toll Tells'?"

"No."

"Oh, you're too young, poor thing."

There was a story to the little plant, though. It was a morning glory, a beach morning glory. Perhaps it would not have made "Toll Tells," but then again, why not? The daily struggle of this weed, the journey, perilous and unlikely, of its seed, the triumph of love, or at least reproduction—these seemed very real to us and crucial when Martha spoke.

"Martha Tells!" Gloria whispered.

Martha talked to us with an easy clarity, which seemed to come as much from her pleasure in her subject as from her actual description. The feeling of being a spectator, a voyeur of nature's wonders, evaporated. Darwin studied dinosaurs, orchids, and his firstborn's smile, not as a spectator, not as a scientist standing above and outside the realm of his subjects. He approached everything, from his account books to the bees in his garden, with a sympathetic, dignified courtesy. It was this trait, I now realize, that we all responded to in Martha. She was positively chivalrous in her studies, eloquent not by virtue of any special quality of language, but by virtue of her own unshakable, irrepressible, courtly delight.

"Look!" Martha said. She pointed to some big brown birds flying low over the water. "Blue-footed boobies."

They dropped to the water like bombs. I tried to see their blue feet, but the light was wrong.

"Will we see the circle of death?" asked the young guy from the plane. His name was Jack Cornwall. He turned to me, boyish and excited. "The boobies make a circle of guano, and the older chick pushes out the younger chick —"

"Booby primogeniture," Martha said. "No blue-footed booby nests today. Soon, though. It's a mechanism for directing resources to the strongest chick—the firstborn, usually, the one most likely to survive—rather than spreading the food too thin and ending up with three sickly chicks. It's astonishing, isn't it? How resourceful nature is."

Mirabile dictu.

"Two eggs are laid and hatched. Sometimes three," Martha was saying. "If there's a particularly abundant supply of food that year, they might all reach maturity. But that's very rare. Usually only one makes it. The oldest one. The others are for insurance."

Primogeniture. An interesting concept.

"The oldest is a little bigger and stronger right from the beginning," Martha said. "It succeeds in getting most of the food. And so it becomes bigger and stronger yet."

"*I* am an only child," Gloria said.

Perhaps in the remote Barlow past, there had been a question of primogeniture—the three Barlows, triplet chicks, trying to grab all the food, trying to push one another out of the family circle, a circle of death, a circle of bright bird lime. The feud could have started there. That was a perfectly reasonable place for a feud to start.

"The parents continue to look after all of their chicks, but the oldest is busy appropriating all the food. The younger chicks weaken from starvation. Finally, the oldest, plump and robust, is able to shove his frail little siblings right out of the nest. He pushes them across the white line. One step across that line and the parents no longer recognize their chicks. The oldest literally pushes them out of the family circle."

The boobies were genetically programmed to fight for their food, to push their own flesh and blood out of the nest. It was a family feud of sorts, an inherited one. The Barlow family feud had been passed along conscientiously from generation to generation, too. Perhaps it was passed along with the DNA. Long ago one brother had shoved another out of the family business, out of the circle of Cuban sugar. The feud was genetic! Martha and I had inherited it!

If this theory were valid, Martha had stopped being my friend because she had to. The family feud had reached down another generation. Martha and I were never meant to be friends. Our families, our backgrounds, forbade it. Ours was a doomed friendship, right from the beginning, as doomed as that of Romeo and Juliet. As doomed as the youngest chick in a loop of white excrement.

There was a tautological aspect to this solution—the feud deciphering the feud. But fate is tautological, isn't it? And so I allowed myself the luxury of imagining the feud reaching, inexorably, through the ages, to pluck Martha from me, to put us at opposite ends of the room, the way our seventh-grade homeroom teacher did.

Martha was telling another story. That was how the natural world confronted her, as practical and complicated and beautiful as a nineteenth-century novel—the life of a yellow, smiling land iguana unfolded in all its Trollopian detail. She continued walking along the beach, pointing out birds and silver crackly plants, her manner both casual and excited, friendly in a bossy way, as if we'd dropped in on her unexpectedly and she genuinely wanted us to stay for dinner. There was something gracious and complete about Martha, the Galapagos hostess. If she had taken out a cigarette, lit it with a gold lighter, and offered us martinis, she could not have been more debonair.

The group walked behind her, everyone politely trying to edge closer, to advance in the line without seeming to, to elbow ahead without offending the competing members of the group. I was no exception. When in the Galapagos, do as the species do. In one brilliant strategic shove, I nonchalantly passed all of the Cornwalls, the multigenerational family of five who stuck together and could therefore, I reasoned, be treated as a single obstacle, thus diminishing my pushy rudeness from a factor of five to a factor of one. This maneuver put me in front of Jack Cornwall (who, even on second inspection, or was it third? was quite nice-looking), and more important, it put me directly beside Martha, from which privileged position I thought about how annoyed I was. No, not annoyed, angry. Annoyed is a mosquito.

Martha looked very much the same as she had when she was sixteen. She was thinner, her skin weathered and tanned, her hair short and bleached by the sun, but the confidence, the tart delight in her own judgment that had marked her as a worthy companion from the first moment I saw her galloping an imaginary horse across her lawn, remained as powerful as ever. It struck me as almost a crime that these attributes had been denied me all these years just because their proprietor had capriciously decided not to be my friend.

As I've said, no one sympathizes when you lose a friend unless the friend has died. I felt myself wishing Martha dead at that moment, partly as a crude and direct expression of anger, partly so that everyone would properly recognize the magnitude of my loss.

"So, Martha," I said. My voice sounded more petulant than I had anticipated. "What *is* a species, anyway?"

What *is* a species, anyway, Martha? It was a challenge, a glove across the face of her leadership and scientific expertise. Drop me and leave me, like a penny, not worth the trouble of picking up, devalued and dull? Well, then, I would ask her the hard questions. I couldn't bring myself to ask any personal hard questions, but I felt that this species problem would do nicely. It had troubled Darwin. It could trouble her.

Darwin gathered slugs and prehistoric skulls and dead birds and sent them off to England where fellow natural history enthusiasts examined them and decided that one was a new species, one a subspecies. But how could they tell? Was the wing of one fly slightly bigger than the wings of its cousins? How much bigger did the wing have to be to make the fly a member of a new species? If the wing differed just a smidgen, then perhaps the fly was a member of a subspecies. Or could it simply be an individual of the same species which varied slightly from its peers, a fly with a big wing?

"What *is* a species?" I said. "And who says so? And how do they decide?" I glared at Martha.

She said, "Your shoelace is untied."

"Nevertheless," I said.

I tied my shoelace with considerable dignity as Martha began to explain genus and family and class.

"No, no, I know, I mean, okay, let's say you're a taxonomist, you classify cacti, you are sent a cactus discovered in Borneo —"

"They don't have cacti in Borneo, I'm sure," said Gloria. "Too wet."

"A cactus from *Tucson* is sent to you. You have to examine it in order to classify it. What exactly do you do?"

"You look at it," Martha said.

I stood beside Martha, warm and comfortable in my resentment. Yet I would not have dreamed of relinquishing my spot, so close to our guide.

"Okay," Martha said. "I think you could say that a species is a group of organisms that have similar structure and behavior, will mate with each other, reproduce, and have fertile offspring."

Jack Cornwall actually raised his hand like a grammar school student, then said, "A horse and a donkey will mate, but they produce mules, which are sterile. Mules are not a separate species. Horses and donkeys are."

I've never liked a teacher's pet. I prefer to *be* a teacher's pet. He gave me a big grinning smile, though, which made his eyes narrow in a mischievous way. Jack Cornwall, like all the Cornwalls on this trip, had a big head, like a senator or talk-show host. He offered me a swig from his water bottle, as if to formalize his definition of species and my acceptance of it.

Martha was by now several hundred feet ahead of us, squatting beside a parched straw-colored stalk.

"No, thank you," I said.

In order to classify his huge collection of specimens from his *Beagle* journey, and to understand natural history better in general, Darwin spent eight years dissecting barnacles so he could learn taxonomy. He peered at barnacles, thousands of barnacles, noting every minute difference. He already knew that variation among individual organisms occurred, and he already believed that it was from these random variations that natural selection took its pick.

Until his eight barnacle years, he thought this variation must occur because of some unsettling, outside event—a huge change of climate, for instance. It was only after contemplating his barnacles, where he witnessed an infinity of variation, where every swirl in every shell varied just a little from every swirl in every other shell, that Darwin realized that variation, the raw material of natural selection, was everywhere.

As we followed our guide across the black rocks, I amused myself by observing the Cornwalls in this way, looking for the genetic variation from generation to generation, wondering what variation might have been favored by natural selection, what variation might continue to be favored. Sometimes I think of natural selection as a large hand that comes and gently lifts a characteristic between its thumb and forefinger, the way a mother dog lifts a puppy in her mouth. Natural selection plucks up the variation, then carefully sets it down in the next generation. I know that natural selection is not a hand. It's not really an action at all. It is a passive record, a picture of what characteristics have worked better than other, vanished characteristics. Still, I imagined a large hand tweaking and smoothing, polishing the Cornwalls, neatly tucking in their common traits.

"Daddy would be so proud of us," said Mrs. Cornwall.

"Your daddy?" said Dot.

"Don't be silly. *Mommy's* daddy."

The family did share one characteristic, it was true: their big heads. Even Brian, the son-in-law, who was not technically a Cornwall at all. Perhaps I should call him the husband, not the son-in-law. But as he was not married to Mrs. Cornwall and was merely married to Mrs. Cornwall's daughter, he was the Son-in-Law. Mrs. Cornwall was the reference point. In her matriarchal wake trailed her son, Jack, who was about my age; her daughter,

Liza, and the son-in-law, Brian, both of whom were in their early thirties; and at the other end of the Cornwalls, the tail end, was Dorothy, Liza and Brian's ten-year-old daughter, a tiny, definite girl, known as Dot. Gloria referred to her as Full Stop. The Cornwalls, who walked in a line, always together, did indeed resemble a sentence, with Mrs. Cornwall playing all the really important parts of speech.

I was walking along the beach, thinking about the Cornwalls but no longer watching them, when I realized I had fallen behind. Only Gloria, my bustling roommate, was with me, the others having moved on. I must have sighed because she patted me on the arm in a kindly way.

"The problem of identifying species led Darwin to realize the transmutability of species," she said. "So it's very clever of you to be confused."

Then she took my picture as I knelt to look at a red and turquoise crab scrambling across the black lava.

` "Sally Lightfoot," I said. I remembered the name from a caption in the guidebook my father had given me. I remembered it because I liked it—a pretty, comical name.

"Sally Lightfoot. *Grapsus grapsus*," Gloria said. "Such a pretty little name, don't you think?"

I nodded.

"*Grapsus grapsus*," Gloria continued. "Just as pretty as a name can be."

There Darwin sat, on his English country estate, his house filled with aquariums, servants, dogs and children, a proper gentleman naturalist, puttering about with his barnacles, peering through a microscope at the swirls of a Cirripedes shells, at the chasm of variation. Amidst his dahlias and governesses and barnacles, Darwin witnessed evolution, read the record of one kind of creature's journey away from its fellow organisms. In his microscope, Darwin saw barnacles that possessed both sexual organs. Then he saw hermaphrodite barnacles with little parasites attached to them. Then he saw barnacles in which those parasites revealed themselves to be tiny, tiny male barnacles. The differentiation of the sexes before his eyes, the birth of sex.

"Taxonomy is profound," I said.

"Yes," Gloria said.

"Did you know that males are really parasites?"

"Yes," Gloria said.

Martha pointed out birds and rocks and plants, as did Jack, who seemed to know his way around, though he had never been to the Galapagos before, but had studied up on the islands so thoroughly that Martha had already begun to stand beside plants, say "Jack," and point to some desiccated stems struggling from the sand. Then she would turn, silently, and look cryptically at the horizon.

"Tiquilia," Jack would say.

"Close," Martha would say. Or, if he got it right, the flicker of a smile would cross her face.

"Jack," she said to him now, pointing to a pallid bramble.

Jack was becoming insufferable.

The storm petrels were diving into the waves and seemed to be surfing. Pelicans, normally so awkward and odd-looking, now seemed gently ordinary, the only familiar objects on that island. We walked over a rise and were met by a silent lagoon. In this gentle quiet, we saw three pale flamingos. We sat on the sand and watched a spiky black reptile. It was a marine iguana, Martha said, our first endemic Galapagos species, the only truly aquatic iguana in the world, large, lumbering, crusty, a crest of chalky spikes rising from its head, running along its wrinkled back. When it lay down, its belly curved beneath it in a paunch, like an overfed cat.

"*Amyblyrhynchus cristatus*," Martha said. "A descendant of the green iguana, the one everybody's brother kept as a pet."

I thought she might be referring to my brother Andrew, who had an iguana named Ignatz, though Martha didn't look at me as she spoke.

"Green iguanas drifted over to one of these islands, perhaps on a raft of vegetation from one of the rivers of the mainland. When they got here, to this barren place, there was nothing to eat. All the animals, all the plants that found their way here, faced that same problem. They adapted to the new environment in some way. Or they died. The green iguana evolved into the marine iguana when it discovered a new, available niche that it was able to exploit. It developed the ability to digest seaweed. Not by changing its own digestive system, though. It digests its seaweed dinners courtesy of a parasite it carries in its stomach. After a marine iguana has baby marine iguanas, she passes the parasites on to her heirs. An essential legacy. An inheritance carried by saliva."

We watched the black reptile lumber away.

"Darwin thought they were hideous," Jeremy Toll, retired gossip, whispered in my ear. "He *always* said so."

A sailor on board the *Beagle* tied a marine iguana to a stone and dangled it in the water from the side of the boat for an hour—a pleasant, boyish way to while away some time, drowning an iguana. Imagine his boyish surprise when he pulled it up and the iguana was as lively as ever. Darwin was a boy, too, when he set sail on the *Beagle*, an unformed, unfocused youth of twenty-two. In fact, there was only one man over thirty on the voyage. One of Darwin's roommates was fourteen. They were boys, all of them, boys playing with lizards, boys straddling the backs of giant tortoises, rapping their shells to make them go.

Darwin, the English lad off on a rugged adventure, did think the marine iguanas were hideously ugly. He thought the Galapagos were ugly, too. They are indeed dry and weedy and bare, neither scenic nor sublime, but scrubby and grim, a place of emptiness.

"But it is a half-finished, rather than an abandoned, desolation, don't you think?" Martha said. "They're like arid island dwarfs that lift themselves from the sea. They look expectant, I think, almost hopeful."

We swam off the beach in water that had made its way up from Antarctica. The equatorial sea was cold and calm, disturbed only by sea lions hoping to play with us. We had all brought our wet suits, snorkels, and masks, just to test them out, and as I paddled along looking at the sandy bottom, I saw Martha swim by me, a flash of black rubber.

I started to say, "It's so cold on the equator!" As I opened my mouth, it became evident that I was sucking on a snorkel, that I was underwater, that I could not in fact speak, that I was coughing and spitting out water. I hastily stood up in the shallow water and looked down at the black form swimming around me.

I said, "I forgot I was underwater!"

Martha stared back at me with huge round black eyes, a snub nose like a puppy, whiskers swaying in the water. Martha wasn't Martha at all. She was a sea lion.

The sea lion shot beneath me. I screamed with all the vigor of a lady who sees a mouse. If there had been a chair to jump up on, I would have jumped. I was gasping, my heart pounding. I was absurdly shaken, as if I had been swimming not with a friendly sea lion, not even with a mouse, but with Moby Dick himself.

Jeremy Toll, surprisingly fit in his wet suit, was standing near me. We looked at each other through our foggy masks.

"It really startled me," I said. I pointed to the sea lion, now doing somersaults between us. "I thought it was Martha."

He spit out his snorkel. We watched the fat, slippery animal dash off.

"I wouldn't tell her that," he said. "If I were you."

In the *panga* on the return trip from our first Galapagos island, there was a chilled, relaxed, fulfilled alertness among the group. We each stared back at the island, shivering silently, aware that we had visited a noble monument, like Chartres.

When we reached the *Huxley*, one of the crew, a tall gaunt young man with a skinny mustache, waited with a hose at the bottom of the ladder leading up to the deck. He grinned politely as he sprayed each of our legs in turn, washing away the sand. He rinsed off our shoes as well, and threw them in a plastic crate on deck, a great mound of shining black Tevas. Grinning indulgently at our excitement, he exchanged some rapid, amused Spanish with Martha. I had refused to learn Spanish as a child. That was my mother's language. I took French in school instead. As did Martha. Señorita Martha.

"Take nothing but photographs, leave nothing but footprints," Martha said, in explanation of the ritual bath.

I watched my colleagues lifting their bare feet into the weak trickle, turning to expose their sandy calves, thrilled to have visited a place so peculiar that even its sand must be purified. One island could pollute another island, and so the patched green hose rinsed away any lingering traces. It was oddly satisfying, a rite of purification, not of us but from us.

I said, "Absolution."

"If only it were that easy," said Gloria.

4

~~~~~~~~~~~~~~~~~~~~

I WENT BACK to my cabin and lay down on my bunk, cradled
in fatigue, the sting of frigid salt water still on my skin. Gloria
stretched out on her bunk, fully dressed, a sleeping exhibit of ecological artifacts. I have read that once an organism starts up the
evolutionary tree in one direction, as much as it branches out and
changes along the way, it cannot retrace its steps or leap over to
someone else's branch. Human beings will change, undoubtedly,
but they will not gradually turn into reptiles, except metaphorically, of course. But Ms. Steinham, as her students apparently
called her, and as she sometimes referred to herself, flew in the
face of this information. She appeared to encompass all the
branches of evolution at once. Her earrings were feathers, her
necklace was shells, her bracelet was seeds. She was adorned with
claws and suede pouches and tiny gourds. Her hat was printed
with tropical fish. Wrapped around her, a cloth of a primitive
African pattern created an ostentatiously primitive skirt. Her shoes
had been woven by an aboriginal Asiatic desert tribe. Her socks,
though, were knee socks and they were nylon. She lay on her

back, her hands folded lightly across her ample breasts, like the stone coffin lid of a medieval queen.

Gloria fascinated me. How could her mother let her go out of the house like that? Her mother was dead. That was the only explanation. I stared at her, and I wondered if I was glad I had come on the trip or not. It was an adventure, as I had hoped. There were boobies and volcanoes. There was Gloria. Even Darwin didn't get to meet someone quite like Gloria. And there was Martha. If Darwin had discovered Martha, I thought, if he had dipped her in formaldehyde and pinned her to a board, what would he have seen? An intelligent, enthusiastic young guide? Or an alienated, cold misanthrope who had moved to a desert and lived in the solitude of crowds of strangers?

No matter how many times I looked back at my friendship with Martha, and at its untimely demise, I could not decipher it. I lay on my bunk, closed my eyes, and tried to picture Martha's face as it now was. Instead, I kept seeing her as a sixteen-year-old, so that when I finally did conjure up the adult Martha, it was hard not to regard her as an old-looking sixteen-year-old, someone who had weathered a terrible tragedy which had prematurely aged her.

I was being ungenerous. And petty. I was quite conscious of it. I was disappointed that Martha hadn't, against all odds, immediately poured out her heart to me. Martha had once defined the world for me. Now that she was a naturalist and guide, it was clear that she would still define the world, at least this little world that I had temporarily joined. Friendship is context, at least ours was. It was what ordered the world. And even though I was an adult myself, even though it had been so many years, even though I had made many friends in the interim, I could somehow not let go of that first real friendship. Particularly when it turned up next to me at dinner.

Martha sat beside me in the dining room, with its large, slightly bleary windows, booths of gleaming varnished wood, and benches of pink leatherette. Gloria and the middle-aged couple named Tommaso sat across from us. I could see from their demeanor that Martha's choice of me as a dining partner, and even her proximity, had elevated my status aboard ship, as if we were dining at the court of Versailles.

"What have you been doing all this time?" I said to Martha. "You kind of disappeared."

"I went to school in Oregon. I told you. Botany."

"No, I meant before."

Martha smiled and looked thoughtful. "Before? Before, I guess I was home."

She went to get dinner, which was laid out on a buffet table, and we all rose from our tables to follow her.

"Pork chops?" said Mrs. Tommaso. "Is that native food or tourist food?"

"Depends on who's eating it, I suppose," said Gloria.

"I didn't know you got married," Martha said to me when we sat down.

"It was sort of a blip on the radar screen. I barely knew I got married."

"My parents are divorced."

"I know. I was really surprised."

"Mmm. No blip, that," Martha said. "Time flies," she said after a pause.

I wanted to say more, to ask more. But Martha had closed up shop. She drank her coffee and read over some notes she'd brought with her.

There are other people on this boat, I thought. I looked at Glo-

ria. It was a good thing visitors were not allowed to remove anything from the Galapagos, I thought, not just for the islands, but
for Gloria Steinham's wardrobe, which was already sufficiently
embellished by all those sticks and stones and bird feathers and
bits of clay she must have picked up on other, less restricted trips.
Because she could not collect specimens this time, she was a most
avid photographer. The thought occurred to me that when she got
home and had the photos developed, she would wear them.

"It's funny that *species* means money," she said.

Species. What *didn't* species mean? But then, what did it mean?
When we had returned from our field trip, Gloria, who in addition
to her remarkable wardrobe had brought a considerable library on
board with her, showed me one book that said the individual, not
the species, was the unit of evolution, and another that said the
species was, but then another warned that a species should not be
confused with a taxon. (This was discouraging. Since I didn't know
what a taxon was, there was every probability that I confused them
daily.) Some scientists thought the clues to a species lay in an animal's form, others in its DNA, others in its ancestry. One group
said that geographical isolation was necessary to form a species, another said that reproductive isolation, not geographical isolation,
was the key. One group said that when we speak of survival of the
fittest, a fit organism is one that is best suited to cope with life's ex-
igencies. That made sense to me. But then another book said that
fit meant reproductive success. A fit organism was one that left
more copies of its genes to the next generation. That made sense
to me, too. These two points of view were said to be at odds with
each other, the basis of a heated scientific feud, so I obviously had
a lot to learn. And what did either view have to do with one branch
of a family tree splitting off from its parent branch, or with one

friend splitting off from another? What did either have to do with speciation, which was the real mystery, the only mystery, the mystery of mysteries?

"Don't you think that *transmutation* is a better word than *evolution*?" I said. "For the mystery of one thing being transformed into another? Evolution sounds so wonderful."

"But evolution is wonderful," Martha said, looking up from the notes she was reading.

"Well, but change is not progress. Necessarily. Change basically stinks. Most of the time."

"Jane's just trying to provoke us," Martha said.

"No, I'm not," I said. I'm trying to provoke you, Martha. But Martha just continued to look at me with a benign and amused smile.

Before coming on the trip, I read somewhere that you cannot tell when speciation is occurring. There is something called a splitting event, but you cannot see the split until after it's happened. You can only look back. You cannot predict the future or even interpret the present. It's not yet clear which slight variation will prove useful, which organism will be favored by natural selection, will prevail over a change in climate or the introduction of some new group into the territory, or the extinction of an old one. Perhaps I had just witnessed a splitting event without realizing it. Martha eating dinner. Perhaps I had seen the seminal episode, a splitting event of tremendous significance: the moment that Martha, now thin, began to get really fat. Years from now, seeing an obese Martha, I would look back and think, *That* was when it started.

I wondered if imagining someone getting immensely fat was a sign of hostility or just envy, because with the rocking of the boat,

I could manage to eat only a little rice myself. I decided it didn't matter because I was entitled to both envy and hostility, considering how unpleasant even slight seasickness was and what a bad friend Martha had been.

"I was divorced once," Gloria said.

"Doesn't that mean you're still divorced?"

"For better or for worse."

Gloria and Martha began talking about lenses and filters, which bored me. It was clear that Martha was not ready to have a heart-to-heart talk, which would not have bored me, so, in the interest of science and camaraderie, I decided to entertain myself with the Tommasos. Mr. Tommaso was a saturnine man, a retired high school history teacher, who was forced to come along with his wife to carry her luggage, though he soon would prove to be the most gung ho of any of us, wanting to crawl into every lava tube, dive into every icy pool, tramp across every field of guano. Mrs. Tommaso was a volunteer at the Humane Society and was therefore quite understandably disappointed in the human race. She was in favor of Nature, though: she seemed to view it, and the Galapagos by extension, as an abandoned litter of kittens.

"Poor little islands. No water for six months."

"I read that two years can go by without rain," Jack Cornwall said from the neighboring table.

Mrs. Tommaso shook her head and clucked. "Such a shame, such a shame, such a shame," she murmured.

I looked from Mrs. Tommaso to Gloria to Mr. Tommaso to Jack and his family, and I felt myself suddenly, rapturously charmed. My heart expanded at what I saw before me: not a cabin full of strangers, but rather, there, in those padded booths, a floating world of curiosities to be collected and labeled in a neat and or-

derly hand. Darwin could not have been more eager upon first setting out in the *Beagle,* or more content upon packing his first fossils to be sent home. Had I really ever cried for a lost husband?
Stuff and nonsense! This group of men and women in many-pocketed shorts seemed so much more appealing than any marriage
could be. Had I mourned a lost friendship? What rubbish. Here
was a whole world, unnamed, uncategorized. Its creatures stood in
a genial line to spoon out their pork chops and rice and squash
from the buffet.

There are certain signals upon which one can usually rely when
distinguishing those individuals who might become one's friend.
"I like your glasses," someone might say. Or you might be wearing
identical shoes. A phrase of unexpected sensitivity or wit is casually thrown into a conversation. Or a haircut will catch your eye. A
nice New York accent on a trip to the Midwest. Or someone on
the bus reading Sybille Bedford. There is a moment of recognition, of hope. Then the courtship dance begins, the chat, the questions, the families and hobbies and prejudices and phobias offered
up for scrutiny. The signals on the *Huxley* were a little muddled—
we were all so out of context, all dressed the same, all reading the
same book. And though my first impressions have proved wrong
time and time again, it was unsettling not to have any. Everyone
blended together at first, a pleasant blur of companionship, a
group of people whose names I sometimes remembered, toward
whom I felt a mild, reassuring condescension.

I turned around in the booth to face the table of Cornwalls.
Mrs. Cornwall was referred to privately by Gloria as La Cornwall
or the Widow Cornwall, for she and her entourage of descendants
were visiting the Galapagos in honor of the deceased patriarch,
Mr. William Cornwall, who had been stationed at the temporary

U.S. Army base on Baltra during World War II and had always planned a trip back to the islands but had never found the time. Jack, Liza, Brian, and Dot all attended the old woman. It is probable that Brian and Dot and perhaps even Liza had a last name other than Cornwall, but if so it was never spoken aloud on board the *Huxley*, at least not in my hearing. They were Cornwalls, one and all. Even Mr. William Cornwall, deceased, had joined the party, the Widow confided.

"We thought we might have trouble in customs," said Brian.

And maybe there would be a seance later.

"Luckily no one noticed," said Liza.

"Like anyone *would*," Dot said with a contemptuous curl of her lip aimed at her mother.

"A spiritual journey," I said politely.

"You could call it that," Jack said.

The spirit of Mr. Cornwall had apparently decided not to join us for dinner, though, for Mrs. Cornwall then said, "What a shame William missed this dinner. He always so enjoyed his meals."

The Cornwalls could be classified as a tribe, I decided. A fairly primitive one. Then there was Jeremy, who would in the old days have been called a lifelong bachelor. But the rest of us came in pairs, like Noah's animals. Roommates Jane and Gloria, two by two. Continuing my shipboard classification, I studied the pair across the room: Ethel, the tall, pink-cheeked, septuagenarian sports enthusiast who knew which way was north and, when asked what she did, said only, "I am a cat lady"; and her roommate, Jeannie, in tight pants, who worked in a doctor's office.

"I've brought an awful lot of medicine, if anyone needs anything," she said. "Compazine, amoxicillin, codeine . . ."

It turned out that everyone had brought large supplies of

medicines and offered to share them with everyone else in a group spirit that seemed to me to hover between that of hardy naturalists and slightly competitive mothers-in-law. Jeannie won the competition.

"*I* have a tooth-repair kit," she said gently.

There was a hush of admiration before we all resumed eating.

Ethel and Jeannie shared a table with Craig and Cindy. This ambitious-looking couple were both lawyers, and they lent an air of youthful success to our group. Craig was about thirty and spoke in a soft but authoritative voice—a voice that had never polluted or even littered, a voice that recycled. Cindy was probably a few years younger, about my age, expensively dressed in the latest gear, and she possessed that smooth, professional air that women who wear hair bands sometimes exhibit. By day, like a comic book superhero, she worked as a steely corporate lawyer. By night, she raised hermit crabs.

"What do they taste like?"

"As *pets*," she said.

I said her name silently, as I did everyone's in an attempt to keep them all straight. Cindy. Then I thought of Noah's wife. When I was very little, three years old maybe, and screaming angrily from the bathtub, my grandmother came in to appease me, as grandmothers do. She sat on the toilet with the lid down and told me the story of Noah's ark. She mentioned Noah and his sons Shem, Ham, and Japheth, and Noah's wife.

"What was Noah's wife's name?" I asked my grandmother.

"Cindy," she said.

In fact, Noah's wife has no name, does she? But my grandmother didn't miss a beat: "Cindy." For years I thought Noah's wife's name was Cindy.

I told our Cindy this story. It seemed particularly appropriate on a boat traveling through the very islands that helped Darwin set the flood story on its ear. People ought to have suspected something was off about that ark business right from the get-go, right at the part where it introduced Noah's wife and didn't mention that her name was Cindy.

"Cindy?" Cindy said. "Not even Cynthia?"

"Jane and I come from a very informal family," Martha said.

It was her first mention that we were not just old friends but relatives, too. Cindy pricked up her ears immediately. Others, too, seemed to have heard and were leaning our way.

"You're related?" asked Jeannie from across the room.

"Distant cousins," Martha said.

The Cornwalls, as the official family on board, looked displeased.

"Wow," said Ethel, which seemed to be the general consensus. Wow, indeed.

On deck that night, I looked at the sky and tried to remember everything I had seen on our first field trip. The air was cool and I had to wear a sweatshirt. I saw the Southern Cross. The Big Dipper was in the wrong place.

I had already climbed into my bunk and turned out my light when Gloria returned to the cabin. I lay in the roar of the engine and the roll of the sea and watched as she stood in the doorway looking at Jupiter's moon through her binoculars. She was carrying a PBS tote bag with an umbrella poking out of it.

Yes, it was good that my husband left me so that my mother could send me on this trip, I thought. There is flora here, and there is fauna. There is Gloria. Martha is here, and she will come around. She will show herself to me eventually—she will rise like the Southern Cross, revolve into sight like Jupiter's moon. This is paradise, this boat and its creatures, all of us engaged in the clear and simple routine of following the leader.

"But why are you carrying an umbrella, Gloria?" I said to the large silhouette in the doorway.

She smiled, patted the long, rolled umbrella affectionately.

"Just in case," she said.

5

THE FEUD between Martha's family and my own was a mystery to me as a child, but in that respect it did not differ from most of my experiences in those days. So much of that time has a hazy quality to it. I don't think that's simply a trick of memory, or a failure, like a failure of eyesight, a mnemonic myopia that blurred what was really perfectly clear. I think the blur is accurate.

My brothers towered above me, exchanging glances and smiles I could not interpret. My mother and father lived in an Olympus of subtleties and nuance. I watched them and I wondered. I wondered about a lot of things.

"If you were a tiny man, as big as a thumb," I said to my father, "and you stood inside my mouth, and I closed my mouth, would you suffocate and die?"

My father stared at me.

"Jane," he said, "I'm speechless."

"'I'm speechless' is speech," I said, somewhat mollified by this linguistic triumph.

I resented that state of childhood wonder. It was insatiable, yet it seemed to me to be no more than a puerile affliction, like baby teeth. My ignorance struck me as a bizarre anomaly, for I felt, with utter certainty, that I was—how can I say this?—that I was *sufficient*. Evidence to the contrary forced itself on me every hour of every day, but that seemed to me some preposterous misunderstanding.

The family feud settled in with the other mysteries of the world. In fact, somewhat more comfortably, for I liked having a family feud in the family, liked the sound of it, the idea of it, possibly because it never occurred to me that I should avoid the part of the family with which we were feuding. I spent every day of that first August with Martha. We did pretty much what I had always done by myself or with my dog. We sat by the stream that ran across both our properties and put our feet in the water. We walked into the swamp and picked mushrooms, planning to save them to poison someone someday, should that be necessary. And we went to the beach. It was a rocky beach, and we had to scramble down a steep dirt path to get to it, but at low tide there was a great flurry of activity there. Crabs sidled around and gulls dropped clamshells on the rocks and terns dove for the bluefish that churned up the water.

Because of Martha's advanced age and her genuine urban sophistication, I was immediately in her thrall. She moved very quickly, without hesitation, and I would sometimes watch her, as I watched many things, in a distracted, openmouthed stare that prompted her to give me a poke, as if to wake me, though I was in fact fully, acutely awake, just stunned by her energy, by the way she tore through a day. I followed her, argued with her, resented her. I suppose it was my own admiration that I resented. I was not in the habit of admiring others, only of tolerating them.

Martha forgave me my resentment. Forgiving suited her. It was her hobby. Perhaps that's why she liked to argue so much. Faults must be identified in order to be forgiven. She prided herself on this generosity. I think, too, that in Martha's eyes, her magnanimity could only be enhanced by her critical nature, for there were always a great many failings and weaknesses requiring forgiveness which came to her attention. There were so many to choose from: even as a child, she had to become something of a connoisseur.

Everyone around us could be counted on for a readily available and rather decent house wine of flaws, but Martha was democratic enough never to slight the daily, repetitive, and ordinary circumstances that required forbearance. And when someone did offer a glorious burst of the unexpected, the exotic, she pardoned that as well. She loved us, and she suffered us gladly.

In the same way that Martha forgave others and continued to love them, she was apparently able to forgive her own weakness and to continue to love herself. It was a trait I envied and tried unsuccessfully, as I did with many of Martha's traits, to emulate. Her understanding of her own essential decency accompanied her so amiably through her life, strong and protective. She seemed as safe as a nun.

We spent week after week walking, sitting, running, and throwing things in all the places in which I'd walked, sat, run, and thrown my whole life. At first, Martha knew nothing about the plants we trampled or the insects we caught. My cosmopolitan cousin listened as I told her that the tadpoles would grow legs and that we might find a mouse's skull in an owl pellet, the full extent of my knowledge of nature, acquired during my naturalist period. She listened not out of interest, though she was sometimes interested; and she interrupted not out of boredom, though she was often bored. I knew that both listening and refusing to listen were gestures, that they were aimed specifically at me, and so I welcomed both equally. They meant that I existed, existed for her, which was the only reason I told her anything to begin with.

We were both bossy, but Martha was bossy in an abundant, inclusive way, while I tended to be merely imperious. Seeing past my magisterial pronouncements and recognizing the limitations of my own nature lore, she quickly filled the gap, taking books out of the library, carrying a guide to plants in her pocket, soon recognizing birds by song and feather, trees by bark and leaves and evening silhouette.

I was stunned by this city energy turned toward my sleepy woods. She had the excessive enthusiasm of an arriviste, and though I corrected her whenever I could, I frequently was reduced to grammatical quibbles, as I was so obviously outclassed in the area of flora and fauna. But when we fought over rules and the meaning of words, like two tiny pedants, our tiffs took on the form of ardent cordiality more than anything else. Until Martha, no one had bothered to argue with me. My parents had smiled indulgently at my intellectual limitations, as if I were a fool or an immigrant who hadn't learned the language yet, or a child. My brothers had veered sharply between telling me to shut up and patting my head. My friends at school cried when I argued with them. But for Martha and me, no subject was safe, no statement, no observation. Was it more dangerous to cross the street at dusk wearing gray or wearing black? We debated for weeks, marshaling our tautological arguments with increasing passion and certainty. It didn't matter that neither of us owned a black garment, or a gray one. It didn't matter that we weren't allowed to cross streets alone anyway. It didn't matter that at dusk Martha had to go inside for her dinner and her bath. It didn't even matter who won. It was during that August, in the midst of our playing and bickering, that I first understood what loneliness was, and understood that I had been lonely, a little lonely, until my cousin and friend Martha Barlow showed up in the country on her imaginary horse to rescue the house next door.

In the beginning, in Barlow, I would meet Martha in the sort of no-man's-land between our two properties. My mother had not forbidden me to see Martha, but I was afraid she might, and I kept a low profile. I did not go to Martha's house, imagining her parents to be as fiercely alienated from the other side of the family as my mother was, and also feeling it would be a betrayal of our side. I asked Martha what she knew about the feud, and she said there was no feud, it was all my side of the family's fault, her father had told her so.

We met at the stone wall shaded by the crooked weeping willow tree. The shadows surrounded us, deep and protective. I realize now that my mother must have known where I was all this time. Or at least whom I was with. But she never let on. Perhaps she thought Martha and I would tire of each other. Perhaps she couldn't think of anything, really, to say about it. It would not have been like my mother to forbid me to play with a perfectly nice little girl next door, even if her ancestors were treacherous criminals. It was more like her to let me imagine that she would forbid me if she found out.

As the weeks wore on, Martha and I sometimes forgot about the feud altogether. Martha would even come and sit on my porch while I went in to get peaches or cookies. Then one day Martha used the bathroom, another day Martha and I watched TV. Then Martha said hello to my mother, who absently said hello back, walked away, turned around, held Martha's chin in her hand, stared at her for a moment, shrugged, and went on her way. After several more days, Martha stayed for dinner. Next Martha spent the night. And so it was tacitly, gradually, agreed upon that the family feud did not have to extend to my generation.

The feud was not even mentioned, except once, when I again tried to bring Martha with us to visit Aunt Anna.

"We don't know that side of the family," my mother said, cold and ridiculous, but quite serious, I could see. Then she told me stories of her childhood in Cuba, which she often did when she wanted to change the subject.

"When I was a girl," she said, "we would go to the market to buy a chicken, and it was not the supermarket, you know, but a big out-door market. My mother would pick out a chicken, a live chicken, and the chicken man would swing it around and wring its neck. We'd take it home in a bag."

I wondered what they did with the chicken's feet, not to mention the head. But I knew enough not to ask, for my mother would have answered.

"Sometimes we'd find an egg still inside the chicken," she said thoughtfully. "With a transparent shell."

After Martha started coming to my house and my mother did not poison her or, more important, embarrass me, Martha took me to her house and introduced me to her pretty mother. From then on, I preferred to play at Martha's house with her mother and the hundreds of objects her parents collected. Mrs. Barlow was an absurdly vibrant, forward-looking woman, always in motion, like a train decked out in crisp chinos and a pink Lacoste shirt. One of her accomplishments was decorative painting. Mrs. Barlow liked to paint flowers on things, and so, as she hurtled through her life, she painted countless flowers on countless things. The Captain Franklin Barlow House was lined with trays and pots she had decorated. Ladder-back chairs. The stairway. The borders between the ceiling and the wall. Even the edges of the shelves in the linen closet. Mrs. Barlow's flowers bloomed everywhere. I suspected that the real reason my Barlow cousins had bought the house was not to rescue it at all, but to give Mrs. Barlow something else on which to paint her flowers.

In addition, Mr. Barlow needed more room for his collections. Mrs. Barlow decorated, but Mr. Barlow collected. He was a tall, slender man with an accent from a thirties movie, an accent connected not to geography but to class, and not even to any particular class, but to a recognition and celebration of the divisions of class. Mr. Barlow actually said "tomahto." He collected Early American tools. He collected model sailboats. He collected tennis trophies, other people's tennis trophies from previous decades.

We did not have collections in my house. At least not any that we kept very long. My brother Fred had gathered up leaves and put them in a book and labeled them, but I drew on them when I was a baby, and they had to be thrown away. I had a shell collection, or told Martha that I did. The truth was, I had brought a few shells up from the beach and left them in the driveway and forgotten about them until asserting their existence two months later to Martha. My mother thought collecting was a bad habit, like coming into the house without wiping your shoes. She didn't collect. She accreted. Our house was full, just uncatalogued.

But Martha's house was different. Within weeks it went from a haphazard group of nineteenth-century rooms, each more in need of repair than the last, to one extensive, miraculous corridor of exhibitions. Every shelf, every table, embraced an aesthetically pleasing drift of objects, all related in some essential way, yet individual enough to suggest ornamental depth and range. There were medicine bottles of cobalt blue and amber and sea-glass green. Little pots that once contained balm or powder, each with an elaborate flourish of a label. One room was lined with paintings of vegetables, another with prints of birds of prey. I would sit on the floor before these shrines, awed, but also suddenly avid. The sheer numbers of things made me want to join in, to add more. I loved the 27 Barlows' house. My brothers always called Martha's house that, as if there were twenty-seven of them over there, and I thought it a fitting name, suggesting variety and amplitude in an exalted platonic sense.

Martha, though, preferred to play at my house. I didn't encourage her. There was nothing in it for me, and I was always a little afraid my mother would forget she was being so tolerant and suddenly turn on Martha. But when we did go to my house, Martha's favorite place to play was my father's study. This was a small room downstairs that was crowded and shabby with papers and books, and only two things stood out in that room: the view and the roll-top desk. From the window, which had no curtain or shade, you could see the verdant crabgrass lawn, the corner of my mother's glorious garden, its lilacs and roses cascading like waves from its trellises and, beyond that, the real waves rolling in from the sea, which itself seemed to have rolled in from the wide sky above. All of this splendor and light and color and constant change from morning to afternoon to night, from summer to fall, from rain to pale wisps of cloud beneath the sun, all of it was framed by the little yellowed room with its big oak desk. The desk had rows and rows of small square drawers that seemed absurdly deep when you pulled them out, like long wooden tubes of papers and paper clips and pencil stubs. Martha and I liked to switch them, exchanging one for another. Then we would wait for my father to come in and work, and if he actually did arrive before we got bored and moved on to something else, so much the better. We would crouch behind the door or in the closet and watch him settle into his chair in that overly elaborate way adults did, then begin to work on papers taken from the mixed-up drawers. He never seemed to mind. In fact, he never seemed to notice, which tells you something about my father's organizational skills. I didn't understand exactly what his work was, only that it involved not-for-profit organizations, the not-for-profit part amply explaining, in my mind, why Martha's family was rich and mine was not.

Most of the time my father worked at an office in the city, but on the weekends he often went to his study and scribbled at his oak desk with the rows of mixed-up drawers. Martha was fascinated by his complacency before such disarray and disorder.

"He just keeps going," she said.

And indeed my father would pull out a drawer, any drawer, examine the contents, and continue with his work, his pen scratching no more quickly, no less surely, no differently from before.

"He just sort of knows where everything is," I said.

"No, no," Martha said. Her voice was impatient. "No. He just uses what he finds."

Martha was very taken with my father, though she was dismayed that I had seen him naked. She had never seen either of her parents naked, or even in their underwear.

"They're just parents," I said. And I was pleased to note that she looked at me with new regard.

My father was always very friendly to Martha, and my mother, though she would never have considered going next door herself and never acknowledged the existence of the 27 Barlows, never snarled at Martha or berated her with stories of her branch of the family's sordid past. I think she even liked her, which was just as well because not only wouldn't I stir without Martha, I also began to dress like her.

I wore a uniform to school—white shirt, blue knee socks, brown shoes, a light blue skirt in summer, a navy flannel skirt in winter. I know some people don't like uniforms, but for me they have always been both soothing and challenging. The uniform relieved me of any responsibility regarding clothing, and yet it allowed me to introduce small variations, thereby signaling some cultural message or other to my fellow uniform wearers.

The evolutionary advantage is pretty clear when birds prance around in their gaudy courtship feathers or insects hide in their dreary splotched camouflage. But what could it mean to the history of the human race that I wore Docksides instead of regular shoes? That friendship pins dangled from the zipper of my coat? That I was able to convince my mother to let me wear nail polish? Nothing, except perhaps to testify to the willfulness of a little girl, surely a great advantage somewhere along the evolutionary line. But at the Charlotte Posey Country Day School, these nuances were important and immediately interpreted. There was a lovely simplicity to the whole arrangement, like a Japanese brushstroke.

At home, I tried to preserve the aesthetic purity of uniform clothing. For that summer, the summer I met Martha, I had adopted as my summer uniform one particular pair of cutoff blue jeans, red high-top sneakers, and my old school shirts. After the first week of vacation, when my mother tried unsuccessfully to tempt me with hideous shorts and sleeveless blouse combinations, no one bothered me about what I wore.

Then Martha came. She offered me what I now understand to be a sort of glorious uniform of the soul, new and intricate and ever-changing, which I could put on each morning without thinking or choosing, which I could wear all day and even at night and revel in the pleasure of the fabric against my skin, the swirl of the skirts, the elegant shape.

Unfortunately, Martha, couturier to my inner self, also wore real clothes. And they were of the kind I had always sedulously avoided. Martha wore frills, outfits, tops and bottoms that matched. There were ribbons dangling from her barrettes. It was everything I hated, her style of dress. And yet I admired her so much I began to relent even on this important matter. This is not to say I gave in right away. We fought endlessly about clothes.

"That's a clown bathing suit," I said, referring to the ruffles on her backside.

Martha just looked at me in contempt, the contempt of someone older and more experienced. "Don't you think it's time you got yourself a new bathing suit, though?" she said.

"No." I approved of the way she had turned my taunt aside and somehow put me on the defensive. All the same, I liked my bathing suit. I had just gotten it the year before, and though I had grown considerably and the red one-piece pulled at my crotch and the straps dug into my shoulders, I considered it my new bathing suit, my grown-up bathing suit, my recognition of propriety, for it was not that long before that I had insisted on wearing my brothers' old trunks.

"I'm getting a bikini," Martha said. "You get one, too. We'll be twins."

Twins!

"There's nothing to hold the top," my mother said when I told her I wanted a bikini. "It's vulgar, a bikini on a child." But she gave in, and I liked the bikini, which was much more like my brothers' comfortable bathing suits than the pilled, stretched-out, and now utterly cast-off one-piece. In the interest of being twins, I then isolated a few select outfits of Martha's that I liked and forced my mother to purchase them for me. One was a sailor suit—blue knit shorts, a white knit shirt with a navy sailor color, and, the *pièce de résistance*, a white beret with a blue band and a red pom-pom. The sailor suit became my new favorite and eventually my new uniform. Martha and I swaggered through the summer like soldiers with gleaming boots and clanging silvery swords. Each time I looked at her, and then at myself, I felt a surge of nationalistic pride. My mother said no self-respecting sailor would be seen in such a suit, but I pointed out that I was not a sailor, I was a little girl.

———

After that first August of our blooming friendship, Martha went back to New York to her school and I went back to my school, where I forgot about her utterly. She receded from my thoughts to make room for a girl named Celeste, who had nostrils that looked like tiny black round coins. Celeste had never been of much interest to me before, and I don't know what happened in third grade, but she came to my house almost every afternoon. Our house had three old maple trees in front, and when they dropped their leaves the ground was deep in color. We made piles, mountains of cold, wet leaves in which we rolled and jumped. In that cool leafy time, Martha was far away, as far away as summer.

My mother took me to school each morning because she taught there. I'm sure that's why I went to the Posey School to begin with. My mother taught Spanish, and she liked the small private girls' school because it reminded her of her school in Cuba, which she said was "innocent, pleasant, and second-rate." My father suggested that as the school's motto: "*Innocenta, placita, et secunda.*"

On the drive there, we would sit beside each other in the car and talk. I would have preferred to look silently at the gray seashore as we drove by, alone in my morning stupor, and she probably would have preferred it, too, but we didn't have that many opportunities to talk to each other alone, and so she would put her hand out on the seat between us and I would put mine on top, and we would talk. She liked to tell me about her garden, especially in the dead of winter when she had no garden.

"But I really do have one," she reassured me. "You just can't see it."

I knew that a lot went on that I couldn't see. And I did find comforting the idea of a garden slumbering patiently beneath the snow, roses buried beneath the drifts. I thought of the roses as living fossils, waiting to be dug up and displayed in the spring. There were plenty of other things buried in Barlow, too, buried even beneath the sea. My mother liked to tell me stories of the ships that had gone down on the reef we could see from my bedroom window. On stormy nights, the rocks were invisible, just as they had been for the ships that she described running across them. I suppose I should have been scared on those nights, but I wasn't. To begin with, I didn't really believe my mother. But even when I thought one of her stories might be true—the tilted masts and jagged tears in the hull, the sailors pulling on ropes stiff with ice, the Barlow residents in their surf boats risking their lives to rescue the crew, then risking their lives to ransack the sinking ships—it all seemed so grand, like something from the Bible. My mother told me Bible stories, too, like my grandmother, and Greek myths, and

I neither knew nor cared which god was from which book, which from Cuba, which from Barlow.

Although my mother was much taken with her marine ancestry, she did not herself ever set foot on a boat. She was surprised when, influenced by Celeste, I wanted to take sailing lessons. My father did not sail either. It was not a sport popular in Brooklyn, he explained, although he did row at Harvard.

"Even Kafka rowed," he said, almost apologetically. I assumed Kafka was one of his roommates.

The winter passed. While I practiced bow knots at bedtime, my mother read seed catalogues to me, which I loved. I thought of my mother and her flowers in one breath, so to speak, as if she were herself a flower, albeit a thorny one. Once Celeste asked me why my mother taught. Instead of saying that we needed the money, that my mother was extremely independent, that she would have been bored to death at home, that any chance to speak Spanish eased her homesickness for Cuba—instead of these reasons, which never even occurred to me, I just said that she couldn't garden in the winter and needed another hobby, which was perhaps the real reason. I don't know. We never discussed it. No one else's mother worked, but it was a given that mine did. I liked her for it, but in those days I liked her for almost everything.

The annoying thing was that my mother liked me for almost everything too. It was difficult to get either of my parents properly angry. I was a sloppy, forgetful, high-handed, underachieving student. I was almost ridiculously argumentative. But my parents just smiled indulgently. We understand, said the smile. It took the wind out of one's sails, all that understanding.

"Dear little Jane," said my mother when I would get angry. "You're actually sputtering."

"You are a girl of conviction," said my father. "I admire that."

Probably part of the reason they accepted me and my despotism with such good grace was that they simply had no energy left, for they fought incessantly with my brother Fred, my adored older brother who was counting the days until he could go off to college. Fred was reading a lot of psychology books at the time, and he told them they were fighting with him so that the separation would be easier. My parents expressed the desire not that it be easier, but that it be sooner. There was often shouting, door slamming, and storming out to the beach for long walks to cool down, in which the participants would occasionally bump into one another before having cooled sufficiently, and the argument would resume.

Sometimes those arguments scared me. But for the most part, I retreated to whatever end of the house was not being used by the combatants. There I would find the dog, Dodger II, who seemed to have much the same idea. We would stretch out on the floor beside each other and I would listen to his breathing, that panting, so beautiful and soft and regular. He would lick my face. And the fight would pass, like the storms.

Some rather spectacular storms swept through that year, one of them knocking down one of our big maples. The waves were enormous and loud, even through the wind. My mother looked out the window at the gray disorder with particular pleasure, I thought.

Once in a while, when I walked past the 27 Barlows that winter, I wondered about the family feud, but not in a very urgent way. It was more of a vague philosophical question, like "Does God exist?" I wondered about God more often than I did about the Barlows. And I wondered about heaven. For instance, would I meet my Grandma Barlow in heaven? And if so, how old would she be? Was there an age that was your real age, even if you never reached it or lived past it: your heavenly age? Perhaps Grandma would be a mischievous girl of eighteen, her hair the same red as in the hand-tinted photograph that hung in my mother's room, her face wearing that same half smile. Would my father's dog, whom I had never met but had heard a lot about, a city mutt who adopted my father and his family and was named Dodger after the baseball team, be there with my grandmother, although she herself had always had a poodle? Sometimes it would occur to me that my father and my mother would die one day, that my brothers would, that even I would. The addition of myself made it so chummy, like a family picnic.

The gray winter sky hung outside my window in the mornings, day after day, broken only by the sudden storms, the rare blue of a sunny day, and the screech of the jays and gulls. I looked out as soon as my father woke me, and he would allow me a few minutes of contemplation before hurrying me to get dressed and eat breakfast. He had told me that when we see, we don't really see the object in front of us: we see light reflected from it. I thought about this all winter, every morning, in those few minutes between being awakened and getting dressed. On my knees on my bed, leaning on the windowsill, shivering from the cold, I wondered what that could possibly mean, our seeing only light reflected, and often poked the glass in front of me, or pinched my arm or tugged at my hair to verify or disprove, once and for all, this proposition.

I was quite philosophical, for those few moments every day, all winter long, until winter began turning into spring outside my window. It was then that I received an invitation to Martha's birthday party in New York. The memory of Martha, the freshness of the springtime air, and the sun, still cold but bright, all blew in my window and made me miss her so forcefully I would have sworn I had missed her every day for months. The card came in an envelope addressed to me, which was already pretty heady in itself. But more important was the return of Martha to consciousness, for she suddenly loomed as large as she ever had, larger—she had become more even than Martha, she had become a New Yorker giving a party on April 12.

I expected my mother to say that birthday parties were vulgar and refuse to take me, but she surprised me. She didn't say a word against the party. She gave me that hug and kiss on the brow which meant that she forgave me, though for what infraction I need not bother my head about.

I did get to go to the party. My father was the one to take me. I wore a beautiful beige knit suit that my mother had gotten for me on one of her own trips to the city. It had a pleated skirt and a jacket with coffee-colored piping and brass buttons. It was from Italy, and I knew it was incredibly chic, even when I saw the other girls in their lace and velvet party dresses. Especially when I saw the other girls, I should say, for I looked at them and thought, in my mother's voice, Vulgar. Even then, I was often overcome by simultaneous shyness and a conviction of my own superiority, and this attitude immediately took over upon walking into Martha's apartment. I stood off to the side, miserable and unable to join in any of the games, and absolutely unwilling to as well. There were a great many of these little girls, a dozen at least. They all looked ridiculous to me, unrecognizable, their faces new and unfamiliar and so somehow inferior. And when I saw Martha among them, she seemed diminished as well. She was fussing with some dolls, and I watched her and wondered that I had ever idolized this plump, conventional person.

Martha looked up at me, smiled, waved, and I waved back and

could not imagine what all the summer excitement had been about. I was furious at her. Surely I could not discuss whether what we saw was real because what we saw was just reflected light with this birthday girl. And I had recently been experimenting with whether one could think of two things at once. I had wanted to consult Martha. For example, did it count if you thought of two people, your mother and father, say, or Martha and me, standing next to each other? Was that two things? Or was it just one, albeit a group, a couple? I had imagined Martha and me sitting together on a sofa, just the two of us, talking the way we used to. But I could see it was not to be, and I almost could not see how it ever had been. I left the birthday party early, telling my father I had a stomachache, disappointed and irritable and prepared to write off Martha Barlow as a lapse in judgment.

The twins had been separated, the branches of the family tree split again, two subspecies of little girl geographically isolated and left to go their own ways. But then June came along, and with it Martha. She burst through our back door as if she'd never been away, as if she'd never lived in a duplex penthouse and played with dolls surrounded by strange little girls. She looked different— taller, thinner. Is this the place to tell you more of what Martha looked like? I think so. Her hair had probably been blond when she was an infant—it was that shade of light brown—and she had odd, narrow eyes that narrowed further when she smiled. Set wide apart, her eyes were an incredibly lucid brown, pellucid is the word, perhaps, for they were quite dark and deep, but also transparent, as if welcoming you into her most private thoughts. Her mouth was large, which I envied, for she could twist it and distort it to great effect. Martha's face had a rubbery virtuosity that did not prevent it from relaxing into real beauty. But it was not the beauty

I envied at that time. Her imitation of a snobbish aristocrat was poetry, her upper lip pulled up in disdain, her teeth revealed in a slight Hanoverian protrusion.

As soon as we saw each other that first day of summer (for the first day of summer, I knew, would from now on occur when Martha appeared), we both remarked on the fact that neither of us wore the sailor's berets anymore or the shorts and sailor blouse. We had stopped independently of each other, and this knowledge drew us closer together. We were both reading Judy Blume novels, and we talked for a while not so much about the content of the books, but about the miracle of coincidence.

Summer was back, an immediate, intimate time of year, when the world was close enough to touch. It was this feeling of freedom, of timeless, shoeless, ambitionless joy that I began to associate with Martha, as if she brought summer with her, rather than the other way around. I can honestly say that for me Martha existed only in the summer. I dismissed the other Martha and all her friends as wintry apparitions. She took on the inevitability of a season. I still thought about the family feud now and then. I associated that with Martha, too, of course. But each year the feud receded further into that mysterious and obscure adult realm to which I was not admitted. It shimmered there and held for me a gorgeousness, like smoking cigars or drinking whiskey, that I preferred to admire from afar.

6

~~~~/////////~~~~

O N THE THIRD MORNING of the voyage of the *Thomas H. Huxley*, Gloria and I got out of bed before anyone else in the group, and we stood on deck shivering, waiting for the sun to rise. We had done this both days before. The wildlife was almost absurd, a child's drawing: sharks in the sea, gulls in the air. Sea lions leapt through the water. Green turtles floated past the bow. Boobies dropped to the water in heavy, perfect dives. Frigates coasted. Fish sparkled.

We watched the birds and the beasts in a kind of daze.

"I don't know where to look first," she said.

Visitors to the Galapagos always report on dolphins frolicking alongside their boat, and Gloria patiently scouted for them. We had not seen any yet, but we spent those early mornings very pleasantly nonetheless, leaning over the rail, talking. There was a great deal to talk about. In our two and a half days, we had already visited four islands and snorkeled on two dark, rocky shores. Gloria could somehow remember on which island each species had been encountered, and had also managed to read three books. I myself was in a feverish delirium of information.

As the sky began to brighten, Martha walked toward Gloria and me and gave a chummy little salute. I watched her, the way she kind of strutted, remembering when we were children, when we were friends.

How do you begin to describe a friendship? Well, let's see: there's mundane, habitual, urgent intimacy. And it's for no reason. I wanted to ask Martha right then why she had stopped being my friend. I wanted to ask her if she would be my friend again. Of course I could do neither. One had one's pride. Anyway, how could she explain the end of something that itself had no explanation?

"What is the evolutionary reason for friendship?" I said to her.

"Good morning to you, too, Jane," she said, laughing. "And evolution doesn't have reasons. It's opportunistic."

I'm sure she knew what I meant, though.

Martha looked up at the frigate birds that hovered above the boat, their deflated scarlet throat sacs just visible in the new sunlight. She smiled at the birds, magnificent black cutouts against the sky, their pointed wings enormous and absolutely still, their long tails forked and stiff in the breeze.

"They don't look like scavengers, do they?" she said.

She climbed the ladder to the top deck to retrieve the wet suit she had hung up there to dry.

I thought, You're very stupid, Martha. I am excellent company. See what a fine time I'm having with Gloria? And all around me on this boat are new friends. Well, perhaps not friends. Friendship might indeed be a deviant, a joke of nature, I thought, when compared with this, the perfect adaptation—camaraderie.

"Darwin had an anthropomorphic side," Gloria continued. She was now reading a biography of Darwin by an Englishwoman named Janet Browne. Her tone was therefore particularly personal and knowing. "Darwin blurred the distinction between man and animal in a charming, gentlemanly, sentimental way," she said. "That's obviously one of the things that helped him overcome the cultural prejudice against an idea like evolution. The English do like their pets."

I wonder if that identification with the animal world was one of the things that drew me to Darwin when I was a child. Perhaps because we are so close to the ground when we are young, because we are face to face with the family dog, we recognize our common humanity, so to speak. When I was five, I told Jennifer of Jennifer Circle, the odious daughter of the contractor who developed the eponymous property across the street from us, that man was an animal, and she began to cry and had to go home. That surprised me, for of all the information I received from my brothers, man's membership in the animal family was the easiest for me to accept—much easier than the secret of sexual reproduction, for example, which my brothers had also revealed to me, but which I did not divulge to Jennifer, not out of delicacy but simply because I thought the boys were making the whole thing up.

Was I insufficiently cognizant of the Nobility of Man? Was that the real reason I accepted this subversive information, which so distressed and still distresses Darwin's critics? Or was it that, as a child, a person of not only lowly physical stature but also inferior social status, I was able more easily to identify with my brothers and sisters of the animal kingdom?

Only someone like Darwin, I think, a member of the ruling class of a ruling nation in its most glorious days of empire, would have the confidence to recognize man's consanguinity with the animal kingdom. Only such a man of wealth and what they used to call breeding, and learning, too, would possess the natural grace and generosity necessary to recognize mankind emerging triumphant from the squirming microscopic jelly at the bottom of his collecting net. And who better to appreciate this imperial Victorian insight into our low origins than a child, both arrogant and aggrieved?

The gradual evolution of each species was one of those scientific ideas that struck me as thrillingly true when I first learned of it, not through its novelty, but through its intimacy, as if rather than first meeting the theory of evolution, I'd recognized it after a long, warm acquaintance. That the world was constantly changing appealed to me, although it raised new questions. For example: How could you be certain of anything? And on a more personal note, if I was shedding skin, which Fred assured me I was; if I was growing, which I could see for myself, then at what point was I me? Wasn't I just a part of me? Or a different me?

A rose was a rose when it was just a prickly stalk in the ground, my mother said, trying to soothe me. A rose by any other name would smell as sweet, my father inevitably added.

"But I'm not a rose," I said.

"And you don't smell sweet, either," Andrew said.

"Changing your name to Rose? That's wonderful, Barlow, dear," Aunt Anna said.

I played the violin for years, laboriously practicing, never really making much progress. Perhaps part of my problem was that as I practiced, my finger slipping a hairsbreadth to distort a G to a something unnameable, I would be thinking, How did the G get to sound right and the something unnameable so wrong? Who says so? In chemistry class or algebra or geometry, the laws of nature were scrawled on the blackboard, as clear as day. But to me, they were as arbitrary, as frivolous, as the rules of Parcheesi.

I told Gloria about my problems with this sort of thing. It was in the nature of a confession. She was, after all, a science teacher.

Gloria explained to me that I was a nominalist.

"Lamarck was a nominalist. The Enlightenment was big on nominalism. You're in very good company. You're wrong, but you're in good company."

In her best science-teacher voice, she explained that a nominalist thinks there are no real divisions of organisms into species, just an endless, gradual arc of individuals. The divisions are no more than arbitrary names given by scientists for their own convenience.

"I'm very radical, it sounds like."

"You? I should hardly think so," Gloria said.

I watched Martha climb back down the steps carrying her wet suit. Then she disappeared into her cabin. She was friendly enough to me, I thought, though no friendlier than she was to, say, Mrs. Tommaso. In a way, I understood and was even grateful. This camaraderie business was nothing to be sneered at—a kind of friendship vacation, all the comforts of home and no cooking! Still, I had occasional unworthy stabs of curiosity about Martha, of resentment and, I must admit, longing. Friendship, that freak of nature, kept limping into view.

What on earth had I done to her, anyway? I went through the possibilities again. And again. Boyfriend interference? No. We didn't even have boyfriends when I knew her. Insufficient appreciation? Hardly. An excess of appreciation, then? Martha had never minded appreciation, and she had been equally devoted to me. General obnoxiousness? An unintended insult? Did I borrow money from her and never pay her back? Nothing I came up with made any sense.

When Darwin and the crew of the *Beagle* first landed in the Galapagos, they were astonished to discover that the birds were so tame they could kill them by hitting them with a stick. I longed to whack my guilty confusion in the head with a stick and watch it fall with a satisfying thump to the ground. We saw albatrosses one day, huge white waddling birds, which may have been what gave me this particular fanciful notion.

"Martha is my albatross," I said to Gloria. Then I realized she could have no idea what I was talking about. And that I had, at that moment, no intention of telling her.

She gave me a curious look. "Maybe you're hers."

"The waved albatross!" I said quickly. "I can't believe they stay in flight for a year at a time."

"Two years," said the science teacher, instantly distracted from any thought of Martha. "They come to land every two years to mate with the same female. A quaint species."

I was confused about Martha, but I noticed that confusion in the Galapagos took on an almost global quality, a grandeur extending well beyond Martha to the creation of the universe itself. This intensity conferred on poor old puzzled uncertainty a dignity, and that dignity was in turn reflected back onto Martha. And so, as I mulled over the problem of species, I recognized that there existed between the origins of life and Martha Barlow an important link: the confusion experienced by Jane Barlow Schwartz. This link was extremely suggestive. It seemed to promise some related solution. If A = (?) and B = (?), then all one has to prove is (?). It was obvious. The mechanism that explained the transmutation of species would explain Martha's transmutation, the transmutation of friendship.

"What is a species?" I said to Gloria.

"Oh, *you know*," Gloria answered.

But I didn't know. The world is an oozing, crawling, swimming, swinging, stampeding, strolling kind of place, reveling in the swarming diversity of its creatures. First we were one, now we are many. Now we are us, and they are spores and pigeons and caribou. How did we come to part ways?

I realize I have a tendency toward analogy. Perhaps you think that unscientific. Again, I point to Charles Darwin, a serious scientist, a genius, a thinker who changed the world forever. He, too, had a tendency toward analogy. In the conclusion to the *Voyage of the Beagle*, Darwin wrote that because "a number of isolated facts soon become uninteresting, the habit of comparison leads to generalization. On the other hand, as the traveler stays but a short space of time in each place, his descriptions must generally consist of mere sketches, instead of detailed observation. Hence arises, as I have found to my cost, a constant tendency to fill up the wide gaps of knowledge, by inaccurate and superficial hypotheses." Or, in his case, accurate and revolutionary hypotheses.

As I stared down into the water, I understood with startling clarity the connection between my revived interest in species diversity and my friendship with Martha. First Martha and I were one, now we were two. We had been twins, then we became strangers, now we were something or other, I couldn't quite put my finger on it. Three days had passed, three exhilarating, rather odd days of endemic species and strenuous physical activity during which, when I had time to think about her at all, I had gone from sullen, leaden anger at Martha to peppier rage to the muddled tranquillity of trailing in her wake, in her knowledge and appreciation of every sapless specimen of Galapagos vegetation, every pebble of volcanic rubbish, every feather, every bob of every head of every bird or beast we encountered. So perfect, so distinct, were the adaptations to that arid, barren land, so perfect and distinct were Martha's tales of nature in all its struggles and glories, that for long stretches I quite forgot she had ever been my friend, I felt so friendly toward her.

"Species," I said to Gloria. "You must tell me. What is a species? That's the mystery of mysteries. Darwin said so."

"He was quoting from someone," Gloria said. She gave an almost inaudible little sigh, an indication of gentle forbearance that made me miss my parents for a moment. "I've always found that phrase banal," she added.

At that time of the morning, the crew were all rushing politely by on their way to raise or lower some huge noisy greasy chain. I thought them wonderfully discreet, for they did not even blink at Gloria, who wore a long, decidedly unethnic nightie, unless you consider New England Puritans an ethnic group. On her arm she carried the PBS tote bag in which she kept her umbrella, tissues, sunscreen, water bottle, the biography of Darwin, a bird guide, and a few Baggies. Around her neck hung binoculars, two cameras, her sunglasses, and a hat.

She started talking about DNA, but as that didn't seem to have any bearing on Martha, and not much on why a husky is not the same species as a wolf but is the same species as a Pekingese—one of my favorite puzzles—I didn't listen too attentively, and eventually it was time to go back to our cabin and get dressed.

Getting ready in the morning was an homage to all that wonderful shopping I had done at home—preparing, donning, arranging everything in the appropriate manner. There was a sensuous, ample significance to each item. Dressing was a whole field trip in itself.

After breakfast, there was a little while before we began shoving off in the *pangas*. I decided to put it to good use by walking round and round the deck, in circles, thinking. Darwin had walked in circles when he thought. Every morning, Darwin would walk along a circular sandy path on a neighbor's property. With each lap, he kicked a pebble onto the track so he would know how many circuits he'd done. I had no pebbles to kick, but I liked the little laps and the idea that it would help me think.

I meant to think about volcanoes, but I didn't know enough about volcanoes to ponder them for very long. So I thought about Martha and species some more. By lap five I got dizzy, and I changed direction, going counterclockwise. That reminded me: Now that I was below the equator, did the shower drain in a counterclockwise funnel? I had forgotten to look. We would go back and forth across the equator during the trip. The Galapagos lie within two degrees of either side. At what point does the funnel of water change? At what point does an individual change to become a member of a new species rather than its parents' species? At what point does anything change? At what point did Martha stop being my best friend? And what exactly was she now? My former best friend? My perfect guide? The object of an obsessive interest born of resentment and hurt? A cold, impersonal distant relative I detested? A vague memory from another era, a fossil stuck in a stripe of sediment?

There. I had thought. Just like Darwin.

Then I got into the *panga* and made sure I sat next to Martha.

She was engrossed in a conversation with Mr. Tommaso about tectonic plates. The earth's crust is like the shell of a hard-boiled egg that has been cracked against the counter, she said, but not peeled. Each piece of the cracked shell of the earth egg is called a tectonic plate. The plates shift around, causing all kinds of crumpling and crushing and piling and stretching. Beneath the ocean floor, there are bubbling pools of hot, liquid rock pushing up through the crust of the earth. The Galapagos were formed when a tectonic plate and a hot spot of spitting magma met beneath the sea. The plate slid across the hot spot; boiling magma from the earth's core bubbled up to the surface. It burst through the crust, through the tectonic plate, a volcanic eruption beneath the waves of the Pacific. The magma cooled and piled up, then it happened again, and again, and gradually a huge mountain poked its head up from beneath the sea. Then the plate moved along, like a conveyor belt, taking the volcanic island with it, dragging a nice fresh expanse of eggshell behind it. The hot spot would again bubble up, creating a new island, and so a chain of islands was born, all riding to South America on the back of a tectonic plate, like monkeys clinging to their mother, the older ones those farthest east, the newest ones, only one million years old, pushing their bald heads up in the west.

"West to east? It's moving *toward* South America?" said Mr. Tommaso.

"It knows what it's doing," said Mrs. Tommaso.

"What *it*?" said Gloria.

"That's the eternal question!" Mrs. Cornwall said with a big smile.

"No wonder the South American governments are so unstable," said Mr. Tommaso. "Islands bumping into their continent every time they turn around."

"You mustn't blame rocks for the follies of our species," Mrs. Tommaso said in her mild, disapproving voice.

"Blame the stars," said Gloria.

Dot Cornwall began humming.

There was a moment during which no one said anything. We watched the island of Bartholome get closer, a squat gray cone.

"An ash cone," Jack said.

"Ashes to ashes," Mrs. Cornwall said cheerfully.

Dust to dust, we all thought.

"The dustbin of natural history," Gloria said instead.

"Quite enough ashes in this place," the Widow Cornwall said, clutching her backpack tighter.

The *panga* bumped against a concrete step. Above rose the cone of ash on its journey from the ocean floor, up into the dry glare of the equatorial sun, east toward Ecuador, then down to the bottom of the ocean again, sliding on its plate down into a huge trench, then slipping beneath the big continental plate of South America. We had intercepted it. Bartholome Island. Land surface: 1.2 square kilometers.

As we jumped off the *panga* onto the concrete steps, we had to be careful not to land on a large, sprawling sea lion. It's undignified to spot a sea lion and immediately begin cooing, as if it were one's brand-new grandchild. But that is what we all did. The sea lion ignored us. It had seen so many cooing tourists. Thank God you are not allowed to touch me, it thought, or you would pinch my cheeks and hug me too tight and say you could just eat me up, I was so cute. We stepped over the sleek mammalian bulk, we gazed adoringly into its enormous dark eyes, we walked up the concrete steps, doting ecograndparents.

The group moved as one behind our leader. Not the arbitrary group we had been when we first boarded the *Huxley*, but this other entity—the comrades. How quickly it had happened. We reached the top of the stairs and stood at the foot of the ash cone.

The doting stopped. The volcanic dust was magnificent, a gentle barren slope, but it was not cute.

"What does Mrs. Cornwall carry in that backpack, I wonder?" Jeremy Toll said softly. "Could it be"—he gave me a sly smile—"Mr. Cornwall?"

Ashes to ashes, Mrs. Cornwall had said. Quite enough ashes on this island. Maybe they really had brought the former Mr. Cornwall to the Galapagos, not just in spirit but in fact, the gray dust of his mortal remains in a Ziploc bag.

"Mrs. Cornwall," Jeremy was saying in a gallant voice. "My dear lady, may I help you with your bag?"

Mrs. Cornwall looked at him as if he were insane.

"I'm quite fit, you know, Jeremy. And why are you calling me Mrs. Cornwall? I don't call you Mr. Toll, though you've got at least ten years on me. Honestly! I'm not infirm. I'm quite fit."

"Ah," said Jeremy. "Then perhaps you would like to carry my bag."

Jeannie, who was wearing short shorts and didn't look too bad in them for an old bat, told Jeremy *she* would love to carry his bag, but he declined. Martha led us up a long, long wooden staircase that the parks department had constructed not so much to aid hikers as to protect the island from erosion caused by hikers. Few things grew on the ash heap: some phallic sprays called lava cactus, each covered with prickly fuzz and tipped with mustard yellow; and a regular scattering of small silver stems, creeping along the dust.

"Jack!" Martha called, beckoning with her finger, then pointing at the weedy growth.

"Vesuvium?" he said.

"Sesuvium," she said with some satisfaction, both at how close he'd come and at how wrong he'd been. "Those tiny white flowers are the only flowers on the island. Have you noticed that all the flowers, such as they are, on every island we've visited, are white or yellow? They show up better at night, when moths come out, when most of the pollination is done."

"I have white roses on my terrace," Jeremy Toll said. "My decorator suggested it. For entertaining at night."

"How Darwinian of him," Martha said.

We climbed to the top of the mountain of ashes. We saw tubes created by lava flowing down the slope toward the sea, its outer crust cooling in the air while beneath it ran on, inside its own tunnel. We saw smaller cones, places where gas had escaped from the main funnel and had bubbled up, leaving spatters, like a messy cook. These were called parasitic, since they lived off the main flow. The great frigate birds flying above us were called kleptoparasitic, because they not only lived off other animals, they stole food from them, crashing into the poor old boobies, causing them to vomit their catch, and then catching it themselves as it fell through the air. We stood atop parasitic cones beneath kleptoparasitic birds.

"Do you think I'm kleptoparasitic?" I asked Martha. I knew this question was tiresome and self-involved. And yet I could not stop myself.

"Do you steal other people's vomit?" she said. "And eat it?"

"Well, only metaphorically," I said.

"That will do," Jeremy said. He said it with some severity.

"Yeah," said Dot. "That's so disgusting."

"Just cover your ears and hum," Gloria said.

"I was just asking," I said.

"I was just answering," Martha said.

In spite of a vagrant, sentimental impulse to revive our ancient patterns of argument, I decided not to resume with Martha the subject of my possible kleptoparasitism.

"Good," Gloria said. "Anthropomorphism can go only so far." She patted my back in the encouraging way teachers sometimes do. "And even metaphor has its limits."

———

Our schedule assumed the inevitable, unchangeable, reassuring birth-to-grave reality of our small town life: we slept as the boat sailed; we woke up on the shores of a new island at 6:30 when Pablo walked by our cabin ringing a bell; we pointed to fish in the freezing water and lizards on the burning ground. We watched sea lion cows nursing their young. Blue-footed boobies whistled at us, masked boobies posed for us, their beaks to the sky. Red-footed boobies watched us from bare white-barked trees. Yellow land iguanas smiled up at our cameras.

"They're so beautiful," Martha would say, gazing at a crusty iguana.

That is why you're a good guide, I thought. You are essentially curious; your enthusiasm is undaunted.

Into this dusty, blissful nature hike that went on day after day, an occasional pang of guilt intruded: I had insulted Martha somehow. Then the pang of guilt was followed by disgust: no, I hadn't; how had I? Then the Galapagos reappeared. Tiny orange-throated lava lizards did tiny push-ups on the lava tuff. Diminutive Galapagos penguins pecked at our goggles. Sea lions, always more sea lions, splashed and dove and invited us, like excited children, to play.

"All the animals are so friendly," Mrs. Cornwall said. " No wonder poor William loved it here."

By this time, I had shed completely whatever initial reservations I'd had about my companions. Who would I sit next to at breakfast? Anyone! With whom would I snorkel, sharing an intimate look, a brief visual exchange, our heads rising from the waves of the Pacific as moray eels slid by us, our eyes clouded by our masks? With anyone! One black-rubber-clad body beneath the steely water was as good as another. Tug on a slippery latex arm, point to the blood-red starfish. Whose arm is it? Anybody's.

"I'm not used to being in a group," I told Gloria. "It's almost liberating. Do you think every group is like this? Should I start going on tour buses to Provence?"

"We are congenial, aren't we?"

"Unless the atmosphere radiates from Martha."

"Perhaps you *should* try a tour bus, dear," Gloria said. "Do you good."

We had sailed that day into a bay surrounded by a huge circle of guano-stained cliffs. We landed at a narrow crack in the cliffs that twisted steeply up the side, a nearly vertical corridor of black boulders referred to as Prince Philip's Steps. The prince had visited this very sight some years back, in anticipation of which these indentations had been banged into the rocks and named in his honor. At the top of the jagged slabs, a level expanse greeted us. The silver palo santo trees were heavy with nesting red-footed boobies, long-beaked white fluff peeping out beneath them. The red of their feet, wrapped around the scorched branches, the blue of their bills, bright as a baseball cap, struck me suddenly as both beautiful and doomed. Surely there was no place for such extravagance in the real world. But this was the real world, wasn't it?

We walked through bare trees, their silver branches rattling with our passage, flashes of red and blue and white appearing on every side. I took pictures of everything, roll after roll, red feet, blue beaks, fluff, masks, and the large nests of the frigate birds, their long hooked beaks hanging over the twiggy edge, their babies tucked carefully beneath them. I watched the boobies as they pointed their beaks to the sky, knocked them against another's beak, picked up feathers and sticks and passed them back and forth, beak to beak. They were courting.

I have a clear, sharp memory of a particularly icy snorkel that afternoon, a beautiful journey of weightless, numb astonishment above pallid sea cucumbers and colorful fish and a magnificently flat ghostly hammerhead shark sliding beneath me in the dark. Dot and Jeremy were partners. They were friends now, too. They had formed a bond, drawn together by a mutual recognition of their shared understanding of and affection for those lesser beings who surrounded them.

"Quite right, too," Jeremy would say when Dot muttered some preadolescent slur.

Cindy was my partner. I had not spent too much time with Cindy on the boat, but I did find her to be a compelling underwater companion. She was an expert swimmer, she dove down with her camera and its strobe flash to absurd depths, she seemed to smell out the biggest, reddest starfish, the longest, whitest-tipped shark, the most dazzling school of angelfish. And she never wore a wet suit! This last fact I found the most wonderful, and I realized I followed her in the water not so much to see the fish she inevitably found, but to watch her not get cold. I followed her until my head hurt from the frigid water, then lifted my face from the shadowy depths to see Sally Lightfoot crabs and snoozing fur seals on the black cliffs above me.

7

~~~~/////////~~~

AFTER SNORKELING, we headed for the *Huxley*'s unlikely Jacuzzi to warm up. The hot tub, which sat on the deck outside my cabin, was really a tepid tub, and it was meant for perhaps three people. Still, when we climbed off the *panga*, shivering in our wet suits, the little pool of lukewarm water could not have appeared more luxurious, and stocking it with ten or eleven or twelve bodies, as many bodies as possible, struck all of us as much more amusing than it probably was. But we had turned out to be, or at least felt ourselves to be, a particularly convivial group. Other groups, when we encountered them now and then on a beach or a rocky trail, struck me as dour and pompous and alien; or, if they, too, were a jolly group, they offended me even more, polluting the islands with their tourist laughter and comments.

"What if I put my left leg under your right leg?" Mr. Tommaso said, climbing into the tub.

"Mine is already there," said Jeannie.

"Well, then, over, I guess."

That afternoon, even Martha got in. She leaned her head back and closed her eyes. We were all still in our wet suits, and they billowed absurdly beneath the surface, full of air and swirling water.

Mrs. Tommaso said, "Martha, why do those poor sea lions have so many scars? Something should be done about it."

Martha opened her eyes and lifted her head just a little. The water bubbled around her throat. "The story of those scars is a love story," she said. "They're dueling scars. You know the big, boisterous male sea lions we see, surrounded by sleeping females? That bull has had to fight off a lot of other bulls to get where he is. He has to continue to fight off challengers, too. And the rest of the time he spends copulating with all the females, one after the other, as they come into heat, over and over again, until he's so tired and worn out that some other male can challenge him, fight him and take his place."

"What an exotic land this is," said Mrs. Tommaso.

"Meanwhile, the females calve," Martha said. "That's all they do for the rest of their lives. They copulate, have offspring and raise offspring, and have more offspring."

"The whole thing sounds like a depraved religious cult to me," Jeremy said.

He stood on the deck beside Dot, his new friend and kindred spirit, both of them watching us in shared, superior amusement.

There were already seven of us in the tub, all women except for Mr. Tommaso. Then Craig and Jack approached the Jacuzzi, and Mr. Tommaso began barking at them like one of the bull sea lions.

"I think that's disrespectful," Mrs. Tommaso said.

"Of whom?" said Mr. Tommaso.

"Those poor male sea lions," said Mrs. Tommaso. "They have so much responsibility."

"Now, here's another Galapagos love story," Martha said. "It's a true story, one that is often mentioned in the guidebooks. But to get this story straight, to be able to indulge yourself in the details of it, to understand its true fascination, to delight in its lacy, farcical intrigues or wallow in its lugubrious tragedy, you would have to do a bit of research. You would have to go to the library and find diaries that are no longer in print, examine old newspapers. Or, better yet, you would have to come on a trip with me, after I had already done those things. You all have chosen the latter path and so I am able to recount to you with some degree of reliability the story of Adam and Eve on Floreana Island."

I had been transfixed, watching Jeannie's impressive cleavage bobbing up and down in the water, but now I turned away to observe Craig and Jack as they tried to climb into the Jacuzzi. Perhaps it was the thought of them as suitor sea lions, but they both seemed suddenly so attractive. Craig was a pleasant muted monochrome sort of person—light brown hair, light brown eyes, regular features, even white teeth, a light brown tan, usually dressed in a beige T-shirt, khaki shorts. He spoke in his soft Canadian murmur. It was a beige accent. There was something comely about him, about how unassuming he was in his looks and his manner.

Jack was quite different. He was small and handsome in an angular way, with his big face and black hair and small blue eyes, which actually seemed to flash. He didn't say much at all aside from his aggressive botanizing and geologizing and entymologizing remarks. And one did have to wonder what kind of a twenty-five-year-old man went on a trip with his mother, not to mention his incinerated father. Either a very weak or a very strong twenty-five-year-old man, I thought. He slid next to me in the hot tub, his knees bent, his arms resting on them. There was no more room in the tangle of wet-suit legs. I noticed we were wearing the same watch, a diving watch.

He gave me his big smile, which made me smile back. I wondered what clothes he wore in real life. I wondered if he had a girlfriend. It was hard to imagine. I could envision him only in camping clothes, on the boat, surrounded by his family, by us. But maybe he'd thought he was going on a different kind of cruise. Maybe he came on this trip to meet girls. Well, there weren't any girls to meet. Except me.

Oh, and Martha. I had forgotten Martha.

"Chapter one," she was saying. "There once was a dentist, a Nietzschean dentist. His name was Dr. Karl Friedrich Ritter, and he really was a Nietzschean of the crudest sort. Dr. Ritter *über alles!* This dentist recognized it as his destiny as a superior person to enlighten one of his patients with the philosophic doctrine of the two of them leaving their marriages and children and starting a new race of super-Nietzschean dentist offspring in an Edenic setting, for the benefit of mankind."

Martha was openly enjoying our attention. She was a good storyteller and like most good storytellers, she seemed to exist solely for the benefit of her audience and simultaneously to find that audience completely extraneous.

"For years, Dr. Ritter and his patient and disciple, Dore Strauch, secretly stockpiled tools and seeds in Germany," she said. "Then one evening, they threw a party for their spouses.

"'We are leaving for Paradise tomorrow morning,' said Herr Doktor Ritter and Frau Strauch.

"'We are?' said Frau Ritter and Herr Strauch.

"'No, not *you*,' they explained. '*Us*. But, we don't want you two to be lonely while we live in Paradise, so we have planned to have you move in together!'

"And they did."

Now, *that* is a splitting event, I thought. Compared to those harsh, overly intellectual, and at the same time Romantic, which is to say Germanic, divorces, my divorce seemed to me suddenly so namby-pamby. And what about the Other Barlows' divorce, Martha's parents'? If most divorces are ugly, I think you'd have to describe the divorce of Mr. and Mrs. Robert Barlow as pretty. Mr. Barlow was incredibly generous to Mrs. Barlow after their divorce, even though it was she who left him, and he continued his genial and unstinting behavior even when he acquired a young wife and infant twins to support. My mother said, with a combination of annoyance and satisfaction that struck me as rather odd, that Mr. Barlow had behaved far better than most men embarking on their midlife nonsense. Certainly he was a better ex-husband than Dr. Ritter.

"Chapter two," Martha was saying. "Dr. Ritter and Dore Strauch decided to locate Paradise in the Galapagos Islands. They settled on Floreana, an island Darwin had visited one hundred years earlier. When Darwin landed there on September 23, 1835, it was called Charles Island. It had recently been populated by several hundred Ecuadorian political exiles who eked out a subsistence diet of bananas and sweet potatoes. 'It will not easily be imagined,' Darwin wrote of Floreana, 'how pleasant the sight of black mud was to us, after having been so long accustomed to the parched soil of Peru and Chile.' The colony of political prisoners had died out by the time the Strauch-Ritters arrived, and there wasn't all that much black mud, either. There was a freshwater spring far in the interior, but most of the island was as arid and parched as anything Peru or Chile could have offered.

"When the Ritters and their several tons of Paradise provisions were dropped on the shore, there was only one human inhabitant of the island—a boy who'd been hired to kill cattle. Cattle, introduced by the earlier settlers, had fared better on Floreana than their masters had, and scrawny bovine herds roamed the volcano's slopes. The boy's job was to shoot them, then drag the carcasses down to the beach for the captain of a local ship to pick up for meat every once in a while.

"But when Dr. Ritter, Über-Dentist and Vegetarian, saw his fellow islander shoot one of the beasts, he was offended on behalf of the cow, and so he beat the boy with a stick. The terrified and bloody boy promised never to do it again, at which point Dr. Ritter stopped beating him with a stick and forced him into virtual slavery. All three of them—Dr. Ritter, the beaten boy, and the limping Dore, crippled by multiple sclerosis but obviously a really good sport—proceeded to drag their tons of belongings up miles of sharp lava boulders to the highlands. There they found a cave carved out of lava by pirates long ago, an orange grove left by the political exiles, and the stream of fresh water. And there Dore and the boy worked, while Dr. Ritter studied Eastern philosophy. Eden."

I noticed the faces of the others—relaxed, but what you would have to call rapt. Martha held them spellbound. She spoke, irresistible and surrounded by water, a Siren still in her wet suit. Why was she able to go on and on with this story about philosophically perverted Germans when she could not speak even a few words to me about herself? The others loved listening to her voice. So did I.

So, probably, did Martha herself. Why, then, could she not turn that voice to the real topic at hand, to the story of our friendship and its untimely demise?

"According to some reports," Martha went on, "the Ritters did not wear any clothes. They did not have any teeth, either, the forward-looking dentist having pulled them all out as protection against tooth decay, and the photographs of them show two mirthless faces with the sunken grimace of the toothless."

I wanted her to turn to me, to talk to me.

"The pioneer couple did find time to write reports of their life in Eden for European newspapers. They became celebrities. Millionaires started showing up at Floreana on their yachts, millionaires bearing gifts. A wheelbarrow. Flower seeds. False teeth made of metal."

The others laughed. They were completely absorbed.

"The newspaper articles also attracted other pilgrims, Romantics who would present themselves naked at the door of the cave and expect to be fed. Poor Dr. Ritter. The cringing clerks had followed him to the bold new world. Most of them, offended by Ritter's cold reception, went home. But one German family, hoping to heal their sickly son, moved to the Galapagos for good, to Floreana. The Wittmers. The new neighbors. The Ritters were horrified—"

I imagined the Ritters' new neighbors in their cave. Perhaps it was identical to the Ritters' cave. Perhaps they turned it into a bed and breakfast.

"Did they open a bed and breakfast?"

"As a matter of fact," Martha said, "yes. Later."

Frau Wittmer had opened a ramshackle hotel.

"Did they have a feud, too?" I said.

"Mmm," Martha said. "A humdinger. Even better than our feud."

"Are we having a feud?" Mrs. Tommaso asked.

"Yes," Mr. Tommaso said.

Martha went on. "Chapter three. The Ritters and the Wittmers began feuding almost as soon as was humanly possible. They argued over the orange groves, the water, whatever there was on the sparse island to argue about. They dutifully fulfilled their vulgar Darwinian destinies, struggling over territory, even over reproduction. Frau Wittmer was pregnant and asked Dr. Ritter if he would help deliver the baby, what with all his dental experience. Dr. Ritter declined to help deliver any babies, explaining that to do so would not be true to his ideal of independence and innate superiority, so Margret Wittmer was left to her own devices, which included wandering up to the deserted pirate cave in a delirium, where she was found several hours later, unconscious and feverish and holding a newborn baby. Ritter felt it was safe to pay a professional visit then, and did perform some sort of surgery on Frau Wittmer, for which she was extremely grateful. When Herr Wittmer offered to pay him, the vegetarian doctor said a year of monthly supplies of potted pork and chicken would do—"

"Martha!" I said.

"Yes?"

"Martha . . ."

"What, Jane, what?" she said in a tone of voice I remembered from my father.

"New neighbors," I said. "Very trying. It was very difficult on my mother, for instance, when our new neighbors moved to Barlow. You know—you. And your family. The Other Barlows. Came and appropriated her town."

Perhaps I said this in an inappropriately intense tone. Or maybe it was simply the comment itself that caused it to clatter so loudly in the abrupt silence that followed. It was a hideous, dropped-jaw kind of silence. The other members of the group stared at me.

"So," I continued, somehow unable to stop, "my father told her that all the starlings we saw everywhere came from a few birds brought here from England by a Shakespeare enthusiast who wanted to introduce to New York City all the birds mentioned in Shakespeare's plays, and that soon there would be Barlows, the Other Barlows, the 27 Barlows, in every tree, on every telephone pole, crowding every bird feeder. So, well, then my mother said, 'That's outrageous. Such things did not happen in Cuba.' And my father said, 'Nor in Brooklyn.'"

Craig did clear his throat, but still no one said a word. By now, they had all turned their eyes away ever so slightly so as not to witness my shame any further. All except Martha. She gazed at me with the subtlest suggestion of a smile and an expression of tender nostalgia. It was an oddly intimate exchange, that glance we shared. It continued, a complete acknowledgment of a perfect understanding, even as Martha burst out laughing.

I thought, You, Jane, are a fool, and now everyone here knows you're a fool. And Martha not only knows you're a fool, she *remembers* that you're a fool.

I thought for one terrible instant that Martha might wink at me.

But she didn't. She just moved on in her story. "Right," she said. "So . . . then the baroness came. She arrived, like Yankee Doodle, riding on a donkey—astride her mount, pistols in her holsters, dark glasses shading her green eyes, dressed like a circus lion tamer. Baroness von Wagner de Bousquet's entourage included two fawning, servile lovers trailing along behind her.

"The baroness proclaimed herself empress of the Galapagos, built a shack out of corrugated iron and called it Hacienda Paradiso, whipped anyone who defied her, and shot at a handsome young visitor who had resisted her charms in order to win his favors by nursing him back to health—but she missed and shot one of her lovers in the stomach. She made a movie about herself, sought financing from North American millionaires for a luxury hotel, received a deed for the island of Floreana after seducing the Galapagos governor's aide, and disappeared with that aide and one of her other lovers. All three of them were probably murdered by the Wittmers and yet another lover who had been recently cast off and frequently beaten, who himself was later found mummified on a beach with a Norwegian sailor. The end."

The end. How convenient for them, I thought.

"It is a good story, isn't it?" Martha said. "Margret Wittmer is still alive. Cheerful old lady. She still runs the hotel, such as it is, and lives there, a little old lady of ninety, greeting tourists. When we go to Floreana, you'll all meet her."

No one winked at me as I climbed out of the hot tub, which was a relief. In fact, the incident seemed to be completely forgotten as soon as it happened. Perhaps they hadn't really noticed my preoccupied, ill-mannered outburst. Perhaps it had never occurred. Perhaps everyone was simply too tired to care.

I took a shower, then stretched out on my bunk to read. I flipped through Margret Wittmer's memoir, in which she accused Dore Strauch of murdering Dr. Ritter. Then, in the interest of fair play, I skimmed Dore's memoir, which Martha had photocopied for us. It was called *Satan Comes to Paradise*, and in it Dore accuses Margret Wittmer of murdering Dr. Ritter. Both of them identify the baroness as a dressmaker from Paris who fled to the Galapagos to escape her debts.

Now, with this image in mind, I think it is time to discuss Paley's argument from design. William Paley was one of those admirable English natural theologians, the parsons who collected beetles and butterflies, who believed the earth was so wonderful and complicated that it had to have been created by an intelligent God who could best be served and honored by study of his marvelous works. Darwin was planning to be just such a country clergyman, until it occurred to him that the force behind the beautiful design of a butterfly was not an intelligent, benevolent Creator, but a history of opportunism, violent struggle, and meaningless accident. In nineteenth-century England before Darwin and his glimpse into the abyss, science and belief went together, as quaint as love and marriage, as a horse and carriage. Because there are butterflies and they are so beautiful and we appreciate their beauty, they must have been made just for us, so that we could enjoy them! We conscious observers are here, the universe is here to be observed, so the universe exists for us to observe, the universe exists *for us.*

Here is my question: Does the spectacle of Baroness von Wagner de Bousquet atop a donkey, one of her lovers bathing her feet in the Ritters' precious drinking water, argue for or against Paley's theory? On the plus side, could there be *any other* reason for the baroness and her six-shooters than our enjoyment of her fantastic, glittering arrival on Floreana Island? On the other hand, how could someone so absurd and unreasonable be *planned,* much less executed, by someone as proficient and experienced as a Supreme Creator?

I put this question to Gloria, but she just said, "Let's think of the baroness as a mutant," and went out to try her hand at fishing off the bow.

I was alone in the cabin, and it was calm and airy. I switched over to *The Journal of the Beagle* for a while, then took up the guidebook by Michael H. Jackson. I lay there contemplating the wonders of Floreana, natural and unnatural, my mind wandering to visions of the other Michael Jackson writing a guide to the Galapagos in his white glove, his stretched-mask face deep in thought, to thoughts of Michael the ex-husband, the details of whose face I found it difficult to conjure up at all. I daydreamed on my bunk, with no knowledge that I was asleep, until I was awakened by the sound of voices outside my window. Two voices, a man's and a woman's, hushed and urgent.

"How much longer?" said the man. I could barely hear him over the roar of the engine. His voice was faint, sincere. "I don't think I can stand it." Could it be Jack? Or Craig? Craig. It had to be Craig. Unless it was Mr. Tommaso or Brian the honorary Cornwall or Jeremy Toll.

The woman replied, though I could not make out any of her words. Her voice was almost inaudible.

"But where?" said the man. "When?"

The woman uttered some indecipherable noises.

"Oh, if only . . . ," said the man. Then his voice dropped even lower. Then I thought I heard him say a name. "Martha."

Was he talking to Martha?

Or about Martha?

Why was Jack talking to Martha and wondering where and when? Why for that matter was Craig talking about Martha and sighing, "Oh, if only . . ."? And what was Mr. Tommaso, a married man, doing? Or Brian? As for Jeremy Toll, he was ancient. Ancient and prissy. He had no right.

The woman replied, her words even softer, even more obscure than before.

"Oh, God, if only everything weren't so difficult," said the man. The voices stopped. I waited a minute. I parted the noisy metal venetian blinds. I looked through the crack. The deck was empty.

It might not have been Martha at all, just someone saying her name. I might even have misheard it. Perhaps they said, "*Mar-velous* weather we're having," or "It's so cold I wish I had a *parka*," or "Have you ever read Sidd*hartha*?"

And what difference did it make if they had said *Martha*? How could it matter to me what Martha did? Martha had veiled herself from me in the filmy contentment of impersonal acquaintance-ship, although she was having a highly personal-sounding assigna-tion with a strange man. That strange man was Jack, whom I had considered making my own particular impersonal acquaintance. So what? Anyway, it might just as easily have been Craig, who was extremely friendly to Martha. But then, so was everyone else. Jack hung around her like the teacher's pet. Of course, he was the teacher's pet. The others came and went, drawn like insects to Martha the candle. She treated them all with the same courteous warmth.

I thought about Martha a lot more than I wanted to. That night, before dinner, I told Gloria I'd heard some sort of assignation be-ing made outside the window.

"Pish posh," she said.

"Pish posh?"

Then, I don't know why, I began telling her about Martha. I ex-plained that she was not just my cousin, not just my friend, but my best friend, my most important friend growing up, that she moved to my town when we were children, that we lived in identical houses.

"But we're different religions," I said.

"You're religious?"

"Well, no."

I was lying down in our cabin, feeling a little seasick and exhausted from our day hiking and looking and snorkeling. Gloria had just showered and didn't seem the least fatigued. She shook out her wet gray curls, put on black culottes with pink rickrack bordering the bottoms and a Peruvian poncho, and said, "Darwin's wife was very religious. She worried that they would not get to be together in heaven because of his theories. That's very sweet, I think. Like worrying that he might catch cold if he didn't wear his galoshes."

Gloria put on a necklace of large shells, which rattled pleasantly when she moved. Her earrings were long dried pods painted a bright orange. The cabin smelled of sunscreen.

"We were such good friends," I said.

The gentle clatter of Gloria's accouterments, the summery coconut aroma of the lotion, the waves, lulling in a large, sickening sort of way, the heat of my own sunburn, like a mild fever—all of it peacefully cradled me.

"But you won't get to go to heaven together," she said, "being different religions and all."

I told Gloria that I used to wonder what age everyone was in heaven. "Like, what if your husband died and then you lived for thirty more years and then you died and there you both were. Would he be your age? Or would he be the age he died at, and you would be thirty years older? What kind of reunion would that be?"

"And now you've had a reunion, you and Martha."

"Sort of."

Gloria came over to my bunk and sat beside me and put her hand on my forehead.

"Fever or sunburn?" she asked.

"Sunburn."

I lay there without moving, except that the boat was moving, swaying and rocking. I wondered why Michael the ex-husband had not worn galoshes. I wondered if Jack did. My father did—big ones with buckles. It seemed a manly thing to do, wear galoshes. How could I have married someone who let his feet get wet in the rain? Gloria meanwhile had gotten two aspirins out of her cosmetics bag. She poured water from a thermos into a glass. I swallowed the chalky aspirins and thought how nice it was to have someone take care of me. Her cool hand had stroked my forehead like a mother's hand.

"Tomorrow you wear a hat, miss," she said.

"And galoshes."

———

I still felt a little sick after dinner and went right up to bed. Gloria stayed in the dining room to hear about the plans for the next day.

"We're going to Tower Island, in the north," she reported back to me. "We sail tonight. We cross the equator around three A.M. I asked Martha to wake us when we do."

"I'm sure she was thrilled."

"And," she said, "Martha made an announcement that the trip would probably be extremely rough."

"Ah."

"She said we should batten down the hatches, so to speak. Well, not 'so to speak' actually, since she *said* we should batten down the hatches and she *meant* we should batten down the hatches. We're supposed to put everything loose away. We can't leave anything heavy on the shelf above the bed, and she said, if you can believe it, to tuck your blanket in really tight to hold you in the bunk . . ."

As she spoke, Gloria was doing all of these ominous things, preparing for our perilous passage north. Only one little light was on. Gloria tucked in my sheet and the slippery polyester satin comforter.

"It's a little rougher up here than below, Martha said. We're farther from the water, we swing back and forth more."

Gloria paused, giving me a chance to respond.

"Well," she said finally. "Sometimes people take their blankets and pillows down to the main cabin below. Martha said to just lie on the floor there. She said it can help. If it gets really, really bad."

"Martha's very considerate."

I struggled out of the polyester mummy, took a double dose of Dramamine, put my head on the flat pillow, pulled the shiny quilt with its orange and purple flower print up to my face, closed my eyes, and fell asleep before Gloria had even come inside from her star watch.

Two hours later, clinging to my mattress as if it were a life raft and failing still to keep myself in the bunk, I lurched toward the bathroom and landed instead in Gloria's bed, though without waking her from a preposterously peaceful sleep. I remembered Martha's advice from her after-dinner briefing and dragged my quilt and pillow down the wave- drenched steps to the deck below. The wind was loud and urgent and the boat had obviously been replaced by a much smaller one while I slept, a tiny little thing as light as a cork that bobbed wildly and without direction, splashed heartlessly about by the bullying dark seas. I slipped on the steps and landed at the bottom with an excruciating thud on my backbone, yanked open the cabin door in the face of the wind, and threw myself and my damp bedclothes inside.

I wrapped myself up in the quilt and lay down on the floor of the cabin. Only the dimmest light came in through the portholes. In the night, the nautical creaking of wood and rope, the clanking of chains, the thud of who knows what landing who knows where, mingled with the sound of the engine beating and throbbing just below my head.

My eyes got used to the dark, and I noticed another lump of blankets beside me. I could not see who was inside. I heard a crash from the corner. That was where a percolator of hot water, heavy white mugs, a jar of instant coffee, and several boxes of tea bags always awaited the weary ecotravelers. A mug rolled past my face. A sailor pushed open the door, stepped over me and the other pile of blankets without a glance, and disappeared into the bowels of the ship. A box of tea bags slid past me. The percolator, quite empty, lodged itself in the small of my back. The door opened again. It was not a sailor. It was a quilt, identical to mine, and a pillow.

"Is that you?" the blanket said.

"Yes," I said.

"No, it isn't," said the blanket in a disgusted voice. It swished past me and went out the door on the other side.

The door slammed shut and the pile of blankets beside me sat up.

"Is that you?" it said.

"Yes," I said.

"It is not," said the pile, then rose from the floor and followed the first blanket.

I pictured the ghostly figures flitting about the stormy decks. At that moment, damp and alone, I wished "it" had been me. Oh, good! the other blanket would have said. Come and haunt the boat with us. Come join us in our revelries!

Another blanket appeared in a few minutes.

"Is that you?" I said.

"Certainly not," said Mrs. Cornwall.

———wwwmmm———

When I woke up, there were six or seven bodies wrapped in quilts huddled around me. Outside, a tropicbird flew alongside the boat, its absurd tail feathers sailing behind it as long and white as a bride's train. But inside, in the weak morning light, no one resembled a lost spirit, or any other sort of spirit. More like steerage class to Tower Island. Mrs. Cornwall had one arm thrown over Mrs. Tommaso, who was snoring loudly. Dot lay curled at their feet like a dog. Jack lay near the door to the galley, Craig not far away. The bundle closest to me was Jeremy. He opened his eyes, then closed them again. I wondered if he knew who had been mysteriously wandering around in their blankets last night. He was, after all, a gossip columnist.

"Jeremy, I saw people wandering around here last night."

"And here we all are," he said.

It was true. Here we all were. A few scattered, sleepy vacationers thrown from their beds by the rough seas of the Pacific. Not a pretty sight, perhaps, but not a mysterious one, either.

"It seemed different last night," I said.

The bodies began to stir. To my surprise, one of them was Martha. She sat up looking a little green.

"And what are you doing here?" Jeremy said, lifting an eyebrow.

"I'm the chaperone."

"It was so eerie last night," I told Martha. "People wandering around like ghosts. It was a little scary. And they kept saying, 'Is that you?'"

"Was it you?" Jeremy said.

"No."

"Not you? Well, that must have scared you, Jane," Martha said.

She smiled and hopped up and was gone before I could think of anything to respond.

"William, you're snoring," La Cornwall murmured, poking Mrs. Tommaso.

———~~~~~~———

When I got back to our cabin, the place was chaotic, things strewn all over by the rough passage. Gloria was wearing a remarkably bright tie-dyed shirt and flowing Indian pants adorned with tiny mirrors.

"I still think there's some hanky-panky going on," I said.

"Well, then, you'd think someone could have awakened me when we crossed the line."

8

⁓⁓⁓⁓⁓⁓⁓⁓⁓⁓⁓⁓⁓⁓⁓⁓

THAT EVENING, I read more of *The Voyage of the Beagle*. Everyone on the boat was reading *The Voyage of the Beagle*. Darwin is a very generous writer, his style welcoming and firm, like a handshake, though I seemed to have an abridged edition that did not include a much marveled-over passage about a dog being skinned.

"Maybe I just haven't gotten to it yet," I said.

"No," Gloria said. "It's not in the Penguin edition. But you have a better introduction."

She smiled, pleased that she had been able to say something nice. "Imagine all the junk Darwin collected," I said. "Barrels and barrels of it. Bones and leaves and tiny corpses."

Gloria sat on the edge of her bunk, still smiling, her eyes dreamy and wide, at the thought of so many natural history trinkets.

Darwin was invited to join the *Beagle* journey because he was a scientifically inclined gentleman, and Captain Robert Fitzroy felt he needed the company of a scientifically inclined gentleman on board or he might go mad, as a previous *Beagle* captain had, as his uncle did, as he himself eventually did, too, scientific gentleman notwithstanding. Fitzroy was commissioned by the Royal Navy to make navigational measurements of little-explored areas. While he drew charts, Darwin filled his nets.

My great-great-grandfather went to Tierra del Fuego not too long after Darwin did. Well, he wasn't really *in* Tierra del Fuego, which was not much of a draw in those days, what with the naked man-eating savages and the cold and all. But he did pass by, as cabin boy on a whaling vessel, round the cape, twelve years after Darwin sailed there on the *Beagle*.

Darwin and Fitzroy were on a scientific journey. My great-great-grandfather was on a capitalistic journey, a voyage to hunt down as many whales as possible, not to study them, but to render their bodily fats in huge fiery cauldrons. While the tectonic plates slid slowly across the ocean floor changing the world, while Darwin sailed the oceans around South America collecting specimens that would change the world, my ancestor was on the high seas blithely committing crimes against nature.

That was the father of the triplets, of Franklin, Frederick, and Francis. He prospered and built his three identical sons three identical houses. He started building them when the children were born, and continued tearing them down and redoing them for twenty years. This bond that Martha and I shared, the murderous whaler and his progeny of indistinguishable F. Barlows and their three indistinguishable houses, struck me as particularly profound out here on Darwin's islands.

"Jane, I think you would be interested in a school of evolutionary thought called cladistics," Gloria told me.

"Sounds like a female reproductive organ."

"Cladistics is concerned only with that moment at which one group breaks away from its parent group," Gloria said. "Ancestors are tracked back through history, through prehistory. Cladisticians are not interested in genetics or populations in their environments or adaptation. They look only at ancestral lineage. Like WASPs from Philadelphia."

"The shabby genteel school of evolutionary thought," I said.

When we trace my family back, we begin like this: me.

Then there is my father. His parents came here when they were young children from different parts of Russia that may or may not have been Poland at the time. Their families settled in Brooklyn.

On the other side is my mother. Her father, Edwin, left the family sugar import business and went to Cuba to work at an agricultural research station. He married his boss's daughter and they had my mother there. The boss's daughter is the oldest of these archaeological artifacts that I encountered in the flesh. She was thin but large-bosomed and carried with her an old-fashioned scent I have never encountered again, an extinct scent. She loved to talk about Cuba, which she had to leave in 1959. She bitterly resented Castro for taking that away from her. "On top of everything," she used to say. And I imagined a pile of things carted off from her house, Cuba tottering on top. She died when I was four. But Cuba remained, in my family, "the Old Country." (And Brooklyn was called "the Neighborhood." Barlow seemed bland and wan compared to these colorful lands.)

My documentation for this point on the Barlow-Schwartz cladistical diagram, my documentation for the reconstruction of Marianne Barlow of Cuba, is a blurry memory punctuated by sudden clear visions of her skinny neck, by the ring of her voice, by a photograph of her, young and dressed in white, in Cuba, in my grandfather's arms, dancing, and by the considerable oral testimony of my mother.

When Martha inexplicably stopped being my friend, I thought of my grandmother and that wheelbarrow of loss, Cuba balancing precariously at its summit. Perhaps that was where the feud had begun. I began to think about the feud a lot then, and it came to seem to me not so much a mystery as an omen, my destiny as a descendant of the Barlows. Somewhere, twisted into the thread the Fates had reeled out for me, there was a coded section as inescapable as a strand of DNA, and it said, "You will dial Martha's number and you will leave messages and gradually, after weeks and weeks, you will realize that she never calls you back." And so it was, so it came to pass, that after weeks and weeks the message-bearer grew tired and dialed the telephone less and less frequently, until one day she realized she had not dialed that number for many, many months, and she was overcome with grief. And rage.

I saw someone die once. I was with Martha. Her family had just joined the Barlow Country Club, and as her mother drove us up the long driveway toward the clubhouse, I could not help but stare in curiosity at the third of the triplet houses, as I did every time I saw it. Inside, it was so different from either of our houses, with its runner of dark red carpeting, as if someone was expecting the queen, and its brass plaques with the names of champion golfers and equestrians, that I almost lost sight of which room would have been which.

On the wet floor of the dressing room plashed dozens of bare female feet, above them their bare female bodies, which looked, from my vantage point and perhaps because there were so many of them, huge and fleshy and draped, as if we were in a vast Rubens canvas, all piled on top of one another.

The two of us changed into our matching bikinis, made our way out through the thicket of naked legs and buttocks, and we spread out matching red-and-white-striped towels on the grassy hill above the pool. We talked, about what I can't now remember, and gazed at the rectangular brightness of the blue water. We saw a man swimming underwater. He swam there for a long time, white and fishlike. We saw the lifeguard suddenly jump in. We saw the man pulled out of the water, saw him receive mouth-to-mouth resuscitation, saw the ambulance drive up, saw it take him away.

Martha and I sat on the hill looking down at death, and while I was curious and shocked and frightened and, so, talkative, Martha was silent.

Sometimes Martha and I were silent together, in a peaceful, ruminative sort of way, like two cows in a barn, asleep on their feet, our feet. But this silence was not like that. Martha didn't even contradict me when I said that I had kissed my grandmother in her coffin (which I had not). When I laughed, out of nervousness I like to think now, but out of a very real ignorance and insensitivity as well—when I laughed and said the dead man from the pool had done the dead man's float, Martha still did not respond. She didn't join me in laughter, which I hadn't expected, for as soon as I laughed, I knew it was out of place. But she didn't correct me, either.

"He was probably really old," I said. I looked at her. She leaned back on her arms. Martha stared ahead of her at the bloated pale white body as it was lifted onto a stretcher, at the one arm that hung down, at the white sheet that covered the man, the corpse, and she was silent, which was beginning to annoy me. We were twins. Why was she so far away, incomprehensible? I remember touching my bathing suit, my twin bikini, as if it would help. Her hands were splayed out on the grass on either side of her. I noticed that her fingers were short and stubby and childlike, just like mine. I gaped at Martha's chubby, child fingers. Death, and the possibility that I would cease to exist, scared me and intrigued me. But as I stared at Martha's fat little fingers, an intense, disorienting feeling came over me, and death shrank away, unimportant, forgotten. I gaped at Martha's chubby, child fingers, and for a moment I saw myself the way other people must have seen me, and I was stunned.

As Martha's mother drove us home, she told me she was sorry we had seen someone die, that death is sad and hard to understand. Martha was leaning out the window, her face flattened by the wind, and didn't seem to notice her mother one way or the other. But I did. Mrs. Barlow patted my bare leg, and her hand felt cool and reassuring, and I wished she were my mother, a soft, gentle presence who thought death was hard to understand. My mother thought death was just fine, in its place, which she reckoned at eighty-two years of age.

Darwin must have thought about death a great deal, although not in the way Mrs. Barlow did, or even my mother. Once, in South America, Darwin was shown an ancient skull, the fossilized head of some extinct, prehistoric monster of an animal. The owner's children used it for target practice and had knocked out all its teeth with stones. I often envision evolution as a world of niches waiting for some enterprising species to jump in. But sometimes I imagine all those others, the individuals of a species who happen to be born with mutations that are only second-rate. They are, in Darwin's terminology, unsuccessful. Which is to say, they die, and their DNA dies with them. Like the bloated man in the pool.

It was an oddly undramatic, distant pageant, that swimming-pool death. But Martha and I never returned to the country club. We switched back to the beach. Martha continued to examine the plants, reading about them, then passing tidbits of information on to me. Queen Anne's lace was really a wild carrot. You could rub jewelweed on a case of poison ivy. The jack of a jack-in-the-pulpit was female. Skunk cabbage smelled so bad in order to attract flies, just the way some flowers smell sweet in order to attract bees.

Each summer, Martha seemed more and more at home in Barlow. The town, named after her family, began to seem to me to be named after her. During her fourth summer in the Captain Franklin house, when she announced that she and her parents were moving to Barlow year-round, it seemed to me a matter of course. I never for a moment wondered why Martha didn't seem unhappy about leaving the city she had lived in for so many years or whether she would miss her old school or her old friends. I knew that such a misplaced nostalgia was impossible. All those pale city girls? A school with elevators? Of course Martha was thrilled to be starting a new life in the robust town of Barlow.

The reason that Martha's parents, Mr. and Mrs. Not Our Barlows, as my brothers sometimes called them, were moving year-round to Barlow was that they had decided to turn their rescued house into a bed and breakfast. Their intentions became clear in August when the sign went up. My mother was appalled that the zoning laws would allow an inn, but my father said that the way the town was headed, the zoning laws probably required the house to become a B & B. The sign was beautifully painted in an ornate script on a large white board that hung from a post at the end of the driveway. "The Captain Franklin Barlow House Bed and Breakfast." My mother was furious.

"We are surrounded by commercial establishments," she said. "I suppose we are expected to open an antique store now."

"Funeral home," my father said. "Beautiful old houses in small towns should be funeral homes. Everyone knows that."

All that interested me about the bed and breakfast at first was that Martha would be living next door the year round. Martha would go to school with me! But as my parents spoke about it, I began to wonder why, really, anyone would want to rent the rooms of their house out to strangers. When I actually thought about all those interlopers examining or, worse, ignoring the Barlow altars covered with treasures, I was baffled.

The only explanation I could come up with was that the Not Our Barlows were short of money. I had long known the story of how my father's parents, Grandma and Grandpa Schwartz, had met in a small town in Pennsylvania. My grandfather had inherited money from a stepbrother, a fact I found amazing in itself, because the only people I knew who had stepbrothers had them because their parents had divorced and then remarried. Divorce was common among my friends' parents, and suggested extramarital sex, so it seemed to me thoroughly modern. Remarriage after the death of a first wife never occurred to me, and I thought my grandfather Schwartz very advanced for having a stepbrother, particularly one who died and left him money.

He took the money and left Brooklyn to seek his fortune. He made his way as far west as my grandmother's little Pennsylvania town. There he struck up a conversation with my grandmother's father, who had come from the Lower East Side and now ran the little town's general store. He also happened to rent out rooms. Naturally, the reason he rented out rooms was that the family needed the money, although my grandfather would later joke that they were really trying to snag husbands for their seven daughters.

My grandfather married the oldest, got bored with Pennsylvania in a matter of months, and continued on his journey, east this time instead of west, back to Brooklyn with his wife.

I had often heard my grandmother Schwartz say how fortunate it was that her family had been poor and so forced to rent out rooms. That was how she met her beloved husband. Every cloud has a silver lining, she would say. Money isn't everything, she would say. Just so you had enough! Then she would kiss my cheek in a horrible nibbling way that was unique to her. No one before or since, thank God, has ever duplicated that kiss.

I liked the story, though. I liked the idea of my old grandmother, the soft folds of her arms crushed against me as she hugged me, the skin on her face loose and delicate against my own—I liked the idea of her falling in love with the handsome young man coming in from his travels. I imagined him looking at her among the seven sisters and knowing right away, recognizing his bride. Of course, he wouldn't know about the horrible nibbling kisses until much later. I had never met my grandfather Schwartz. He died before I was born. But I had seen pictures of him, and I was a little in love with him myself. I agreed with my grandmother. How lucky to have been poor and forced to rent out rooms and so be swept away by a handsome stranger.

Thus I thought the Barlows, like my paternal grandmother's family, must have fallen on hard times. And like my grandmother, they didn't seem to mind. One reason they didn't mind was that no one ever came to stay at their bed and breakfast. Except me. There was no handsome stranger who swept into their lives to marry their lovely daughter. There was just the girl from next door. Martha and I were allowed to choose any room we wanted, and we migrated from the one with violets on the wallpaper to the white bedroom with the canopy bed to the one with the fireplace and patch-work-quilt–covered twin beds. My mother, needless to say, was delighted that they had no customers and scornful of my own participation in what she called "the flophouse."

"The flophouse that flopped," she would say.

That sounded sweet to me, like the title of a children's picture book. But my mother's continued animosity upset me. It was so unfair, I told her. Martha hadn't done anything. Even her parents hadn't done anything. Not to my parents. Or to me. "This feud is so stupid."

But all my mother said was, "Don't be silly. That is the nature of a feud."

Mr. Barlow had retired early in order to start the bed and breakfast with his wife, and I got a chance to know him a little better than during those previous summers when I'd only caught glimpses of him on his way to or from the train station. His wife called him Barlow. When I told my mother, she began to call my father Schwartz and he called her Schwartzita, but that lasted only a few days. Mrs. Barlow always called Mr. Barlow Barlow. He was tall and had an awkward elegance, like a shorebird, his long legs moving with an unlikely grace. His accent, which as a child I thought was English, was really an anachronistic boarding school drawl. He clearly loved the sound of his voice, which was, indeed, a pleasant instrument, and he spoke in his lilting, mannered way with great frequency and generosity. He was a kind man, outgoing and charming even to me. I was quite taken with him. He was so different from my gruff, funny father. And the only suggestion that this man and my mother were cousins was their eyes, an icy blue, which were astonishingly alike. My mother, cool and slim and quiet, who moved with a light quick determination, who never seemed to be at the center of what was happening, but seemed always to be above it—could she really be related to this man who would stand chatting with a twelve-year-old about Northeast Harbor?

"The Wallaces have a splendid house just up the road from the Abbots, but they won't spend a bean on it! Do you know them? Rich as Croesus, old Campbell Wallace."

"Why won't he spend a bean, then?"

"I can't imagine. Lovely town, though. That's where I met my wife. Sailing. You don't sail, do you, my dear? No, I wouldn't think so."

"Why not?"

"Well . . ."

"I wanted to learn to sail. But my mother —"

"Yes. Quite. She never did sail, did she?"

"Did she?"

"Sailing is marvelous. You must take it up, you know. I haven't been in years."

Martha and I discussed this disparity between the two Barlow cousins and felt that probably somewhere along the line there had been a mistake, eyes or no eyes, that one of the two was not really a Barlow at all. Perhaps someone had been adopted.

"Or else he takes after his mother," I said.

But Martha didn't know if he did or not. Her grandmother had died before she was born.

When Martha asked Mr. Barlow what his mother had been like, he said, "Mother was a suffragette," and began to cry.

———————

"Maybe this will end the feud," I said to Martha on our first day of school together, the day we began seventh grade.

"The feud was about love," Martha said. She spoke with great authority, as she always did. "They always are."

"Money," I said anyway. "Daddy said it was business."

Martha shook her head in that pitying way she had. "There's a love child somewhere back there," she said. "I guarantee it."

I asked my mother if there was a love child in the family and she snorted.

"Where did you hear that? How very nineteenth-century."

"Maybe it was *in* the nineteenth century," my brother Andrew said. "A secret love child. Or maybe it's *you*, Jane."

"Stop it, Andrew," my mother said.

"I'm sorry," Andrew said. He gave me an affectionate pat. "I forgot. Jane is *adopted*."

"*You're* adopted," I said. "You don't look like anyone." Which was not true. He looked just like my mother. And just like me.

"You're both adopted," my mother said.

And for a moment I wished I could be adopted by Mr. and Mrs. Barlow. Then I would be Martha's sister. And go sailing.

Since this was clearly not to be, I consoled myself with the knowledge that at least Martha had moved to Barlow for good, which was how it should be. The town assumed the dimensions of reality itself when I was a child. I was born in Barlow, and I assumed I would live there always. Barlow was so enduring, so loyal, repeating the names of members of my family reverently on street signs. Barlow Highway. Three Captains' Drive. I watched my mother's garden die each fall and return to life each spring, and that's how Barlow seemed to me. Changes occurred, but they didn't really change anything at all. There was a quarry when I was a child, an abandoned quarry, in which we would swim. We weren't allowed to, but it was fabulously deep, and we could dive off the high sides and keep going down into the dark icy water. The quarry later became a neighborhood of fancy houses, back to back and belly to belly, no sign left of the deep, delicious water hole. This development outraged me when it happened, but then I remembered that the quarry itself had not always been a quarry. Before it was dynamited for gravel, the quarry had been a mountain.

I often thought about my family's past when I was growing up. The feud was tantalizing, naturally, but all kinds of stories about the Barlows and the Schwartzes had been recited and joked about and contradicted and denied and asserted and told and retold ever since I could remember. "Puss in Boots" and "Cuba" and "Grandpa Schwartz and the Seven Sisters" and "Jacob and Esau" and scraps of unintelligible Spanish were the bones and skulls and fossil teeth of my childhood. Gloria was right—cladistics was just my cup of tea.

"Yes," Gloria said. "But cladistics is too limited. Now, I have my own theory about you and Martha. You see, organisms change over time, individual organisms, and some of the features that are useful to them when they are young are not of any use when they are older, and some features are only of use when they mature and must begin to court and find a mate. In an analogous way, there are features that were once of value to a species that are no longer useful, and so these features have grown smaller or changed function or even disappeared. You see?"

She stood up, looming above me, her arms crossed. "That explains Martha, dear. Doesn't it?" she said. "Martha Barlow is a residual organ."

Martha a residual organ? Martha is a thumb, I wanted to say. Something essential, defining, not residual. When the last of Grandma Schwartz's sisters died, Grandma sat in a chair with a bewildered look and said, "Who do I tell things to?" Whenever we children did something cute, she would smile and then tears would come to her eyes. "Who do I tell?" she would say softly. "I don't have my sister to tell."

"You don't like my theory, do you?" Gloria said.

"No."

"Do you have a better theory?"

When we would ask my sixth-grade science teacher a question, she would always answer, "Because God made it that way."

"Because God made it that way," I said. "Martha is not a vestigial organ, and if she is, it's because God made her that way. For our enjoyment. I'm converting from nominalist to natural theologian. You have driven me to it. I want to be a country clergyman. I want to be given a living and grow dahlias. I want to catch butterflies and hold jumble sales. Did they have jumble sales in the nineteenth century? Or is that only in Barbara Pym novels? I think of Martha as a sort of echt friend. You see? The model on which all other friends must be based. And so this entire shipload of strangers has partaken of her essence."

"Oh dear," Gloria said. "You're not a nominalist. You're not even a natural theologian, really. You're a silly old essentialist!"

9

We were a calm, heterogeneous group, a stagnant pond of little girls, before Martha came splashing in. The urban rhythms of her speech, her nervous city pace, distinguished Martha in our poky school. Not only was she blessed with a profoundly advanced taste in pop music, but Martha also had a boyfriend in New York whom she had kissed. At an age when most people hate to stand out, Martha flaunted her singularity.

She said, "Girls, I'm here to corrupt you."

With determination and energy she led strikes and sit-ins protesting our having to wear pastel dresses to dance around the maypole.

My aunt Anna had moved in with us by this time, when her housekeeper finally died, and she and Martha soon became great admirers of each other.

"Your little friend shares our family appellation," Aunt Anna said after I brought Martha up to her room to meet her one morning.

"Well, she's a Barlow," I said.

"Is she? Perhaps she's related," Aunt Anna said.

"She's my cousin," I said.

"Is she? Perhaps she's some sort of *cousin*, dear," Aunt Anna said, smiling.

"Your aunt is so great-looking, like a flapper," Martha said later the same day.

"She thinks you might be related. Because of your name."

"I want a strand of pearls like that, long."

"Maybe she'll leave them to you in her will. If she remembers you're related."

It was amusing having Aunt Anna live with us—*she* was amusing. The stairs were difficult for her to maneuver by herself, so I was often called into service. I would stand in front of her, one step below, as she leaned on my shoulders. Step by step, slowly, slowly, we would make our way down the stairway.

"Maybe it would be easier for you if you moved into a room downstairs," I said.

"Oh, no, Barlow, dear," she said, breathless, her hands clutching at my shoulders for support. "I like my independence."

Most of the time, Aunt Anna stayed in her room upstairs dressed in an old silk dress and the long string of pearls, a cigarette hanging from her trembling lips. My mother would bring her breakfast up there. Graziela, a young woman from Cuba who was staying with us to help out with Aunt Anna, would bring her lunch. But every evening, at five sharp, Aunt Anna called me to help her downstairs for cocktails. Five o'clock was cocktail hour, even though she would then have to sit down in front of the TV and wait for an hour and a half until my father came home from work and mixed her a martini with two olives. They would clink glasses, say "*L'chaim*," and relax together in silence for half an hour or so. My father loved Aunt Anna. Finally, there was someone who understood the importance of a stiff drink and a moment of repose after a long day.

"You're a highly civilized woman, Anna," he would say.

"Nonsense," she would answer. "I'm not the least bit high. Hollow leg, you know." And a long ash would drop from her cigarette to the floor, landing as lightly as an angel.

When she discovered Graziela could drive, Aunt Anna began inviting her out for lunch.

"Come along, Gracie, come along. Hamburgers!"

Sometimes I would bump into them when I stopped at the diner for a doughnut on my way home from school. Aunt Anna had introduced Graziela to the pleasures of tobacco, and I would see the two of them in a booth, hunched over an ashtray and crumpled red packs of Winstons, their smiling, animated faces in a haze of blue smoke and rapid Spanglish.

"Now," Aunt Anna said on one of these occasions. "English lesson! I teach you. Should anyone ever give you any trouble about anything . . ."

Graziela looked baffled.

"If, well, let's say, you, Graziela"—she pointed to Graziela—"unhappy." She made a sad face. "Bad man bad to Graziela."

Graziela stared intently at her teacher.

"*Anyone* bad to Graziela, Graziela say: 'Son of a bitch.'" Aunt Anna pronounced it very carefully and slowly. "Son of a bitch."

"Ssahn ahf ah beech."

"A regular native, my darling."

Graziela had been a seamstress in Cuba and was saving her money to open her own shop. She was supposed to clean the house and cook dinner for us, but what with the hamburgers and English lessons and the dresses she was sewing for Aunt Anna, my mother, and me, there was little time left for extras.

I came home from school early one day—it was a half day because of teachers' conferences—to find Aunt Anna hanging on bravely to the vacuum cleaner as it dragged her old frail person in violent, loud bursts around the living room.

"What are you doing? You'll kill yourself," I said. I turned the machine off and gently pried Aunt Anna's bent fingers from the handle.

"Extraordinary machine," she said.

Graziela came out and said Aunt Anna wanted "to go hamburger" in a new dress that still needed to be hemmed, and when Graziela had protested that she really did have to vacuum, it was after all her job, Aunt Anna had offered to do it while Graziela finished sewing the desired outfit.

"Graziela! Hamburgers!" Aunt Anna said suddenly, jumping up, teetering for a moment until Graziela ran forward to steady her.

"Now she is forgotten," Graziela said.

"Now she *has* forgotten," I said.

"Nonsense," said Aunt Anna. "Graziela remembers everything, don't you, dear? Extraordinary," she added as they passed the vacuum cleaner and swayed unsteadily out the door.

My mother had great faith in Graziela and often bemoaned the fact that we did not have enough money to get her started in her own business. But Graziela did what she could from her room, which housed an astonishingly diverse expanse of pins, rolls of material, paper patterns, and scraps that piled up like colorful leaves. One of her most devoted customers was Martha. Martha had changed from the days of ruffles and bows that so enraged and fascinated me, and Graziela kept both of us in an abundant supply of clothes. When we tired of preppy blouses and skirts and turned to layers of thrift-shop silk and lingerie, Graziela magically transformed these items into clothing that fit. I loved this constant manufacturing in the room downstairs, though I was studying the Progressive era in school and worried that we might be running a sweatshop.

"Now that's a good idea!" said my father, who was getting a little tired of making us cube steaks every night for dinner because Graziela was too busy sewing and we too busy being fitted. "Clever girl." He patted my head.

Just in case, I suggested to Graziela that she might consider unionizing herself. But the mention of unions reminded her of Castro, and she said, "Son of a bitch," very loudly, slowly, and with a perfect accent. She returned indignantly to her sewing machine.

Her English teacher put down her martini and applauded loudly.

"By George, she's got it," my father said, and went to the kitchen to make us dinner.

For nearly three years, Martha lived next door, Aunt Anna lived upstairs, and Graziela sewed. "Mmm! Pins for dinner!" my father would say, observing the state of the dining room table. "And thread!" My mother drove me to school each day. Martha's mother drove her to school. My mother also applied to the zoning board to have the Not Our Barlows' Bed and Breakfast closed down. She called the Wildlife Federation and reported destruction of natural habitat. She wrote letters to the local newspaper in which she complained of the strain on the sewage system, though the house had a septic tank. The Barlows, in response, wrote letters to the editor emphasizing their contribution to the local economy. My mother, in response to their response, wrote a letter complaining of the traffic brought in by the bed and breakfast. The bed and breakfast, meanwhile, had not had a single guest.

Then, on a beautiful spring day at the end of ninth grade, when leaves had just begun to show themselves on their dark, wet branches, when the wind blew in from the sea with a new, fresh scent, when the sun shone down as if in eternal benevolence, our house burned down.

Martha and I saw the smoke as we walked home from school. We had just smoked some hashish she'd gotten from one of her old friends in New York. The sweet, sticky smell clung to us in that brisk fresh air, and we moved sluggishly down Barlow Street toward a great, black billowing cloud.

"That's my house," I said.

I ran the rest of the way and got there in time to see Graziela helping Aunt Anna down the porch steps, one by one, slowly, slowly. The dog stood behind my aunt, nudging her gently but deliberately with his black round nose.

"That's my house," I said again. I saw Martha running to her own house. I wondered if she was calling the fire department.

Aunt Anna had a cigarette dangling from her lips.

"That's in extremely poor taste," I said.

"Winston tastes *good*," she said. "Like a cigarette should!"

I could already hear the sirens as we walked to the edge of the lawn. I tried to think what of value might be burning up in the old white house. I thought of my father's papers in his wonderful old desk. I thought of Graziela's dresses and scraps of dresses. I wondered if the heat would wilt my mother's roses in the garden. I imagined the melted CDs and dripping black vinyl, formerly Grateful Dead albums.

Martha came and stood with us.

"I called the fire department, and I called the headmistress so she could tell your mother."

She looked down at the ground. I realized she was embarrassed, as if she were looking at someone with a deformity.

"At least it wasn't your house," I said. "With all those collections."

Martha looked up with a start, and then I knew that she had been thinking the same thing.

My mother's car roared up the road. She had beaten the fire engines.

"What happened?" she said. It was the obvious question. But I had not been able to bring myself to ask Graziela and Aunt Anna, for the answer also was obvious. My mother looked at Aunt Anna, the cigarette dangling from her lips, the long ash falling to the ground as lightly as an angel. She looked at Graziela, Aunt Anna's protégé, and at her cigarette dangling from her lips. "Oh God, oh God," my mother said. She shook her head. "Are you okay? Are you all okay?" She didn't expect a response. She turned from us to the house.

The firemen were there. They were rushing in and out of the door. They were carrying heavy canvas hoses. They rose gracefully into the blue sky on long ladders.

By the time my father got home, the fire was out. It had started in the living room, probably from an ash smoldering all night in the cushion of Aunt Anna's favorite chair. The fire itself had been put out before it spread through much else of the house, but the smoke and water damage was enormous.

We stood on the edge of the front lawn and looked at our wet, blackened house as the sky darkened around it. Aunt Anna sat with Graziela in my mother's car listening to the radio. She liked Madonna.

"This young woman has spunk," she said, nodding her head in rhythm.

For a moment, I thought of the day, years before, when Martha and I had seen the man in the pool drown.

"You'll have to stay at our house," Martha said suddenly.

My mother turned to her in horror. Then I saw it dawn on her that one of the results of having your house burn up was that you had no place to stay. There were no hotels in Barlow. There was one disreputable motel that had hourly rates, which I wasn't even supposed to know existed. And that was about it. Except for the Captain Franklin Barlow House Bed and Breakfast.

"Do you have any vacancies?" I said, and Martha and I began to laugh uncontrollably. The flophouse that flopped had never had a single customer. Barlow was not a place tourists visited. Mr. and Mrs. Barlow never seemed to mind, though. In fact I think they were relieved. Guests would have disturbed the aesthetic equanimity of their bed and breakfast.

The hash had by now worn away almost completely, but combined with the situation of the fire, it left me with an eerie, lightheaded sense of unreality. Martha and I could not stop laughing once we started. We laughed and laughed. My mother and father stared at us.

"Let me see your eyes," my mother said. "They're all red."

"Mom!" I said indignantly. "It's from the smoke. There's been a fire. Remember?"

"I called the headmistress," Martha said, somewhat irrelevantly.

"Yes. Thank you, Martha." My mother smiled and gave a little laugh. "She came to my room, and said, 'Ladybird, ladybird, fly away home! Your house is afire!'"

"And so it was," my father said.

"Ladybird, ladybird!" Aunt Anna said in delight.

We all headed over to the Captain Franklin Barlow House Bed and Breakfast.

Martha went in ahead while Graziela and I herded Aunt Anna up the porch steps. The dog, my mother, and my father followed. At the threshold to the house, where I had stopped so many times to marvel at the orderly twin of our ramshackle house, where I used to stand in awe and murmur "Chaos," my mother now stood. I heard her say, very softly, under her breath, "Shit."

"Think of England," my father said.

The dog lay down on the porch.

"Think of England," my father said to him.

Mr. and Mrs. Barlow greeted us formally, as guests, as tourists passing through who had unexpectedly but gratefully come upon this charming inn where they hoped to be able to rest before continuing on their journey through New England in the glorious springtime.

"Welcome!" Mrs. Barlow said. "Can we get your luggage?"

"Mom!" Martha said.

"I'm Robert Barlow," Mr. Barlow said, holding out his hand to Graziela. "Everyone just calls me Barlow."

"Barlow is right over there," Aunt Anna said, pointing at me. "Don't I know you, young man?" she added.

"Of course you do," my mother said. "That's Robert. Hamilton's son. Hello, Robert. Thank you for taking us in on such short notice. It's rather an emergency, or we would not have presumed —"

"Why, you're Robert!" Aunt Anna said.

"I'm so happy you have chosen to stay with us," Mr. Barlow was saying to my mother. "It's been such a long time. You look wonderful, Vanessa."

"*Who's* Robert?" Aunt Anna said.

"You actually know each other?" I said. "I thought —"

"*I'm* Robert, Aunt Anna. Do you remember me? I haven't seen you since I was a little boy."

"I had a little cousin named Robert, you know," Aunt Anna said. "Nice child."

"That was me."

"Was it? Pity about his parents. Shocking, really."

My father grimaced and took Aunt Anna's arm and led her into what he knew would be the kitchen. "I think you deserve a cup of tea, Aunt Anna. You've had a big, incendiary day, haven't you?"

I wondered how it was, if there was this longtime family feud, generations of Barlows not speaking to one another, that my mother actually knew her cousin Robert Barlow. And watching my father trying to distract Aunt Anna, I couldn't help but wonder some more. I saw him exchange a glance with my mother.

"My poor brother," Aunt Anna went on. "Wouldn't change, you know."

"Who?" I asked. "Grandpa Edwin wouldn't change?"

"The sheets!" Aunt Anna said.

"Or a drink," my father said, still trying to steer Aunt Anna toward the kitchen. "Would that be all right, Mrs. Barlow?"

"Never got over it," Aunt Anna said.

"Who never got over what?" I said. "What sheets?"

"Jane," my mother said. "*Cállate,*" which meant, basically, shut up, and was one of the few Spanish words I understood.

"Vodka," Aunt Anna was heard to say as she was steered into the kitchen. "Two olives."

We had a family conference in the driveway in front of our smoke-blackened house the next day. The builders had already been there and estimated three to four weeks to clean it up. My mother was furious.

"How can I force poor Aunt Anna to stay in that awful place?" she said.

"Under the circumstances, I think the old firebug deserves it," said my father. "Anyway, it's quite comfortable. Charming, really. But it's you I'm worried about."

"Oh please."

"The sheets are clean, at least."

My mother shuddered.

School ended, summer began, and still we were guests at the Captain Franklin Barlow House Bed and Breakfast.

Aunt Anna's muddled condemnation of Robert Barlow's parents reminded both Martha and me of the family feud. We had long ago given up our speculation regarding love children and the like. The economic explanation was quite satisfactory, we had decided, now that we were grown up and cynical. But here was this new information. If you could call it information. Aunt Anna had dangled it before us, shimmering scraps of some larger, gaudy tapestry. "Wouldn't change," Aunt Anna had said. Who wouldn't change? Martha's Barlows? And what wouldn't they change? Their wills, obviously. Had Aunt Anna been cut out of the wills of Hamilton Barlow and his wife, the suffragette?

"And what sheets was she talking about? What do sheets have to do with wills?"

"Sheets of foolscap?" Martha said. "Or bedsheets, stained wedding-night bedsheets."

"*Un*stained wedding-night bedsheets!"

"Adulterous, incestuous bedsheets!"

"Hence the love child."

"The half-wit love child."

And we pointed accusingly, gleefully, at each other.

I went over to our house one afternoon to watch my mother garden. I liked it there. The house was sooty and decrepit in places, freshly painted in others, and the garden billowed up around it. My mother had never been a more assiduous gardener than now. It was quite literally the only time she felt at home.

"What was Aunt Anna talking about? What sheets?"

"Oh, the sheets."

"So, like, the sheets of a will? I didn't know you knew Robert Barlow when you were younger."

"Didn't you?"

My mother's face was hidden behind branches of pale lilacs and dark leaves. Her shears clicked now and again.

"The sheets," she said from behind this floral screen. "They really could have changed the sheets. It would not have been all that much trouble. Aunt Anna went to stay with the Barlows, with Uncle Hamilton and his wife."

"The suffragette."

"Was she a suffragette? I can imagine her marching. She was a marcher."

I waited. It was everything I could do not to interrupt, to reach in and steer the story back to its course. But I sensed that I had caught my mother at a good time, lulled by scented purple blossoms.

"Aunt Anna went to stay with them. With Martha's grandparents. They showed Aunt Anna to her room, which was Robert's room when he was home from college, and they said, 'Oh, Robert only spent two nights here. They're as good as new.' It was all a big mistake, all of it, the whole thing, a hideous mistake, but I was young, and I thought—oh, who knows what I thought, or if I thought at all in those days. Young people are very stupid, aren't they, darling? Poor things. Not you, of course."

"They didn't change the sheets? And Aunt Anna is still upset? That's so bourgeois."

"Well, it wasn't a hippie commune, was it?"

"Dirty laundry," I said. I sneered, too, a very satisfying sneer, with a curled lip. "It's so *literal*."

"Yes," my mother said from behind the lilac. "Dirty laundry."

———

Martha and Aunt Anna and Graziela and I spent much of that summer sitting on the lawn behind the house in lawn chairs smoking cigarettes. Aunt Anna was no longer allowed to smoke in the house. She sometimes forgot, and we would smell the tobacco from her bedroom and hurry in to stub out the cigarette before one of the parents found her out. In return, she let us bum Winstons off her. It was an idyllic summer.

My mother adjusted to the situation by going to her garden early each morning and returning early each evening. That way she was in the house as little as possible, and her roses bloomed fatter and more content than ever on their trellises. She planned new plots, planted new bushes, pruned, weeded, dug, and scraped in a happy delirium of horticulture from morning till night. The garden, bursting gloriously from the earth, looked even more beautiful in contrast to the rickety, patched-up house. In the afternoon, my mother would take a break and have a swim at the beach before returning to her calling. She got an incredible tan.

She did participate in our innkeepers' breakfast, though. Even

Aunt Anna came down for that. On the first morning at the bed and breakfast, there was a short power struggle, as Graziela and my parents tried to help out in the kitchen, and Martha's parents insisted on serving us breakfast as if we were regular customers. I suppose we were. We, on our side of the feud, had insisted on paying the regular nightly rate for our rooms. But that first morning, we all felt a little uncomfortable and tried to help serve and clear up. The Barlows wouldn't hear of it. They were insulted. They were indignant.

"We are professionals," they said.

My mother sat in glowering humiliation as Martha's parents brought us fresh-squeezed orange juice.

I thought it was quite nice to be served breakfast, and to have breakfast with my best friend, Martha, who by virtue of her tender age counted herself among the guests rather than the hosts.

"Stop smirking," my mother said to me.

"Will you have our breakfast special?" Mr. Barlow asked. "On Tuesdays it's pancakes and homemade blueberry muffins! Or would you prefer cereal?"

My mother bit her lip.

And so the days passed. Aunt Anna obviously felt at home, for she began to pin little notes to all of Martha's parents' furniture.

"Nivea," a note would read, flapping from the back of an armchair.

"Left heel on pumps," said another. "Nota bene."

My mother would slip out of the house after breakfast, and arrive back only to load us into the car to go to the Chinese restaurant or the Italian restaurant for dinner. She was coldly polite to the Barlows, who were coldly polite back.

My mother grew more and more tan and robust. But Mrs. Barlow, perhaps by contrast, seemed to grow more and more pale. Her face looked drawn. Her smile, so full of energy and direction in the past, had faded into a halfhearted grimace. She didn't get to spend much time outside, what with the laundry and cooking and cleaning for her guests. Her garden suffered. She no longer had time to paint her decorative borders. Now, rather than a locomotive of womanly progress, Mrs. Barlow seemed more like the desperate and weary Little Engine That Could. Up the mountainside she labored, day after day.

Mr. Barlow, always gaunt and patrician, became more gaunt and patrician.

"Of course you remember the Boston Wilburs, marvelous people, not the Chicago Wilburs, you know, they died years ago. And their *son*, well—such fun, the Wilburs. But I don't know if you ever stayed at their place on St. Barts. It was she who gave us this recipe, wasn't it, dear?"

"Delicious," my mother said, taking a bite of a huge, fragrant muffin. It was clear to everyone that by this time she had reconciled herself to being served by Mr. and Mrs. Barlow, had in fact come to enjoy having her enemies wait on her hand and foot. "You must give my compliments to Mrs. Wilbur."

"Of Boston," Mr. Barlow said, clearing away the plates of bacon and eggs.

"And of course to Mrs. Barlow," my mother added, bestowing on that person a triumphant smile.

"Of Barlow," my father said.

"Thank you," said Mrs. Barlow in a tight voice as she poured my mother's coffee.

"Well, you know," Mr. Barlow said, "not for long, not for long."

"What's not for long?" Martha asked.

"'Of Barlow.'"

"All good things must come to an end," said Mrs. Barlow. She went back to the kitchen.

"Yes," said Mr. Barlow. "The Captain Franklin House Bed and Breakfast is closing."

There was silence. My mother gasped in alarm. Then she must have remembered her campaign to close the inn. "Oh!" she said. "How . . ."

"Ironic?" said my father.

"Horrible!" I said.

"Daddy, what are you talking about?" Martha said.

"Your mother and I have decided to move back to the city."

Aunt Anna took out a cigarette. No one stopped her. We heard the snap of her lighter, a beautiful gold lighter, and the click as it closed.

"At the end of August," Mr. Barlow said. "Our guests will be back in their house by then, I'm sure."

My father started to say something, but Mr. Barlow interrupted.

"We were happy to be available to our guests, even more so as they are relatives, and we'll still come out for summers," he said. "Of course. But this country life is, well —"

"What? Is what?" Martha said.

"Well, *suburban.*"

I tried to take in what I had heard.

We had driven the Barlows out of Barlow.

My mother was uncharacteristically quiet, a little smile playing over her lips.

We have driven the Barlows out of Barlow! she was thinking.

My father watched her for a moment, not sure what she would do or say.

We have driven the Barlows out of Barlow, he was thinking. What will she do or say?

My mother did and said nothing.

My father began politely and sincerely thanking his estranged cousins-in-law for their hospitality and skilled innkeeping.

"I don't know what we would have done without you," he said.

"Tents!" Aunt Anna said.

Martha and I were staring at each other as the news sunk in. We had driven the Barlows out of Barlow. Martha was a Barlow. Martha was moving back to New York.

"Shit," Martha said.

"Martha!" said her mother from the kitchen.

"Like the flowers that bloom, we shall return to our lovely patch of rustic green each spring," Mr. Barlow said.

"I thought it was so suburban," Martha said.

"Like the vernal ponds that appear each year, teeming with life, then disappear, only to return a year hence —"

"They're full of salamanders," Martha said.

"What are?" I said.

"Vernal ponds. They're really just puddles," she said to her father. "And I hate metaphors. They're lies."

"Yes, I hate to lie in a tent, too," Aunt Anna said. Then she looked at Martha's father. "Don't I know you from somewhere?" she said.

———

Martha and her family moved back to New York City at the end of August. We moved back into our house. I hardly had time to miss Martha, the house needed so much sorting out. It had been painted, inside and out, and the furniture had been cleaned, but the smell of smoke still hung on. Clothes had to be thrown away, papers sifted through. It was during that frenzied two weeks of cleaning before school started that I discovered a paper bag with a few old letters in my mother's closet.

"Love letters?" I said.

"Really, Jane. Are they even mine? Some old papers."

"So!" I said. "At last! The real explanation of the family feud."

"You loved that feud when you were little, Jane."

"I didn't *love* the feud."

"You were adorable."

"When you were little," my father said.

"You thought there were murders, wasn't that it? Something very Latin and dramatic."

"A love child," I said.

"Yes, well," my mother said.

It was an odd and sparse assortment. A postcard from someone named Geoffrey in California; several unsent birth announcements for Jane Barlow Schwartz, with little pink ribbons at the top; a photograph of my father with no shirt on; and, last, two letters from my mother's father, Edwin Barlow, in Cuba to his mother.

The day he arrived in Limones, Edwin sent a letter home announcing he had met the family of Professor Linden, the Harvard botanist who had recently set up an agricultural research station there. The Lindens were exceedingly hospitable and courteous, he wrote, and Professor Linden was delighted to have Edwin as his new assistant. The next letter discussed Professor Linden and his dream of improving the sugarcane and making new varieties through crossbreeding which could be marketed to cane growers and so prove profitable. "He came to Cuba hoping to produce a hardier race of cane by crossing vigorous types with weaker canes of high sucrose content." The professor, Edwin wrote, had arrived in the winter a few years before when he had undertaken to study the floral structure and fertility of the cane flowers and find a suitable location for an experimental station. "Limones was selected," he wrote.

Limones was where, a few years after this letter was written, my mother was born. It was a town that was a garden named after a fruit. As a child, I used to say the name of my mother's birthplace over and over, and I could almost smell the blossoms of the lemon trees, though I had never seen a lemon tree, much less smelled one, and had no idea if lemons even grew on trees. They could just as easily have grown on bushes or vines for all I knew.

My mother had told me stories about Grandpa Edwin and Grandma Marianne, how they had been thrown together, the only two foreigners of their age in the town.

"Work on the garden was commenced in the fall," Edwin wrote.

"This tells me nothing," I said to my mother.

"Nonsense. It tells you that in the past, work was such a beautiful thing that it was 'commenced' rather than 'begun.'"

"Oh, Mother."

"Work on the garden, as if it were the Garden of Eden. 'Work on the garden was commenced in the fall.'" My mother smiled in an annoyingly beatific way.

In the Garden of Eden, Eve ate an apple and gave some to Adam and everyone knew what had gone wrong. But what had gone wrong for the Barlows in their garden of lemons and sugar?

"So why was there a feud if everything was so wonderful in Edenic Cuba?" I said.

My mother kissed the top of my head in her gesture of compassionate acquittal. "Didn't Adam and Eve have a quarrel in Eden? That's what Eden is all about."

Aunt Anna died in the hospital the year after Martha left Barlow. She had a heart attack. I was at school. My mother was at school. My father was at work. Graziela, Aunt Anna's smoking buddy, called the ambulance and rode in the back with her, holding her hand, and murmuring "son of a bitch" over and over, like a prayer.

Aunt Anna was in the hospital for about a week.

"Graziela sews," Aunt Anna said the next day, looking up from her hospital bed. "And she shall reap!"

She laughed at her joke, but she was paler and weaker than usual, and without her clothes and makeup and cigarette, she looked bare, like a tree without leaves. The doctors had told us she might pull through, but looking at her stretched out and unadorned, I thought that unlikely.

"Graziela is Cuban," Aunt Anna said.

"My mother is Cuban."

"Graziela is *not* your mother, Barlow, dear."

"No, she isn't."

"I visited your mother in Cuba. Your mother was a little girl, you know. A lush and verdant island. The fragrance! Sometimes I think of what I've seen, what I have even now. And then I think of where I'm going. To the grave. In a hole in that dirty dirt."

"Oh, but —"

"Then I say to myself, Anna Barlow, if Princess Grace could go in that hole in the ground, so can you."

"But Aunt Anna —"

"And then I say, Anna, when you get there you won't know your ass from your elbow anyway. So shut up."

She smiled at me. She offered me a cigarette, tried to light it for me with her trembling hands.

"The Barlows grew sugar in Cuba, right?" I said. "Or imported it?"

"Sugar is the root of all unhappiness," Aunt Anna said with a sudden vehemence that surprised me. "Sugar killed my father."

Slowly I worked my way through the family ties, as I always did when anyone dead was mentioned. Aunt Anna was my mother's aunt. She was my grandfather's sister. She had visited her big brother, Edwin, at Limones. So Aunt Anna's father was my great-grandfather, Frederick. The other two triplets were her uncles. Martha's great-grandfather Franklin was Aunt Anna's uncle.

"So he had, like, diabetes? Hypoglycemia? I thought Great-Grandpa Frederick died of a stroke."

Aunt Anna sighed heavily. Two scrawny arms, as white as the sheets they lay on, reached out. Two bony hands grasped my arm.

"Never repeat what I am about to tell you," she whispered.

"Okay."

"It could place someone in grave danger."

"Right. I won't tell."

She pulled me closer, put her mouth to my ear.

"Graziela," she said, cackling with pleasure, "is bringing my martini at five o'clock!"

"God bless Graziela," I said.

"God? Pshaw!"

"I thought you were going to tell me something about the feud."

"The feud . . ." she said. She trembled. Her voice trailed off. She closed her eyes. I had a terrible feeling that she would die that very moment, the secret of the feud dying with her, killing her actually, with its cursed power of generations of hate and bitterness.

"Aunt Anna, just rest. Don't talk now. Never mind that stupid feud. Should I call the doctor?"

"Those dirty hypocrites," she said. She opened her eyes. She raised a frail fist. Her voice was clear and vigorous. "Vultures. Gangsters."

Dr. Bradley a gangster? He was a white-haired gentleman who wore big, square space shoes.

"They killed my father," she said. She shook her finger at me like a bird waving its long beak. "Sold off parts of the company, said my father owed the company money. They kept the profits, you see? From the sale. Left him with nothing. Not even a job. We never talk about it. They say his hair turned gray overnight. But I remember it black as night. He died soon after. Poor as dirt."

I stroked her arm.

"Edwin left Harvard, went off to work. Employed by that professor fellow. Poor Edwin. Poor Papa. Sold the company out from under him. Said he owed them money!" she said.

"Did he?"

"Oh, yes," Aunt Anna said. She smiled serenely. She reached toward the bedside table and patted her hand absently over the surface, searching for the pack of cigarettes.

Martha took the train out and saw her the next day. I heard this from Aunt Anna. Martha did not call me. She had stopped calling. She had stopped returning my calls. Aunt Anna died three days later.

The funeral was small and sad and in a church. Martha didn't come, but her family sent flowers.

"Garish," my mother said when she saw them.

10

~~~~~~~~~~~

O<small>N THE SHORES</small> of the Galapagos Islands, I had begun to pose questions to myself not only about the mystery of creation, or even about the mystery of friendships and feuds, but now also about the mystery of hanky-panky. Visions of bodies draped with blankets wandering across the midnight cabin like spirits on a moor plagued me.

Perhaps I was just an old gossip, like Jeremy Toll. Or a phrenologist, those contemporaries of Darwin who judged people's characters by the shapes of their skulls, who saw meaning in the bumps on their heads. I reminded myself that not everything means something, that some bumps are just bumps. But still I daydreamed and speculated idly the way I always had. I thought, If only I could have followed those fleeting forms. But they had vanished, lost in a crowd of seasick passengers waking up on a varnished floor. Of course they must have been the same couple that had met outside my cabin window and whispered their need and desire.

"Where? When? Oh, if only . . ."

I envied this furtive couple the hush of their secrecy, the urgency of their voices, their intimacy.

"My ex-husband was a horse's ass," I said to Gloria. "And now I'm too disgusted to find a new one. He ruined everything. Martha's a horse's ass, too. Perhaps it was she who ruined everything."

Gloria furrowed her brow. She tapped her forefinger thoughtfully on her cheek. She fixed her eyes on me as if I were another bone or leaf she might study.

"I think," Gloria said, "that you are the common denominator in those two equations." Then, in a schoolmarm voice, she added, "Let sleeping dogs lie."

"My mother used to say, 'Lie down with dogs, wake up with fleas.'"

"There you go," said Gloria. "You can't keep digging up a friendship like some chewed-up old bone . . ."

At the word "bone" she looked suddenly concerned. "Jane!" She turned her back to me. "Look at my spine," she said. She twisted her head around to me, her brow furrowed. "Calcium deficiency?"

I was sure she was not deficient in calcium. I was sure she was not deficient in anything, and I told her so. Nevertheless, she went down to the galley to see if she could get a glass of milk. I stood by myself, beneath the morning sky, and realized how little time was left. I tried to imagine going back, but it seemed quite impossible and thoroughly unnecessary. I saw a head pop up from the stairs, thought it was Gloria, hoped it was Martha, and realized it was Jack. He saw me, smiled his rather dazzling smile in a way that suggested to me that he knew it was a rather dazzling smile, and came over to stand beside me, both of us leaning on the rail.

"Don't you love being so far away from everything?" he said. "And everyone?"

"But your whole family is here with you."

"I meant you."

"But your whole family is here with me."

Jack kept an eye on his mother. I noticed that. But he didn't follow her around or fetch and tote for her. This was a delicate balance, surely, and required an emotional surefootedness, even grace, or elegance. I wondered what it would have been like to have my mother on the trip. She would have kept an eye on me, I suppose. Certainly, there was nothing she could complain about as vulgar. I thought she would have been happy on such a trip, which made me feel for a moment how happy I was.

"Yes, you're right," I said to Jack. "I really do love being so far away."

Later that morning, I took a picture of Jack. He was standing beside a mangrove. It was a profile, his head turned to face a red-footed booby perched in the tree, also in profile, the two of them staring absurdly at each other. And at lunch, I sat with all the Cornwalls, all except Dot. She was at Martha's table.

"It's so stupid," I heard Dot say. It was what she often said. "It's so stupid to try the *preserve* the Galapagos. Evolution means, like, change."

"It is sort of stupid," Martha said. "Now that you mention it."

That's what makes it noble, I thought. Or is that what makes it stupid?

"My niece is very wise," Jack said, and I realized he had been eavesdropping, too.

We spent a lot of time together that day, Jack and I. He was my snorkeling buddy, pointing out different kinds of coral and fish. If he wasn't as good a guide as Martha, he did focus all that he did know on me, and that goes a long way, doesn't it, all that undivided attention? Galapagos penguins kept diving in with us from a rock, like lemmings. There weren't very many of them, maybe five, but they dove in one by one, stared at us, then waddled back out onto the rock and dove in again. I don't think they were playing the way the sea lions did. They seemed piqued.

When we got back to the *Huxley*, I beat Jack, and everyone else, to the hot tub, but even as I lowered my frigid limbs into the warm water, Jack was climbing in beside me.

"Those penguins," he said, "those minuscule penguins. Didn't you find them threatening? Like the old ladies with their shopping carts at Fairway?"

"You shop at Fairway?"

It turned out we lived on the same block in New York. My number was 401 on West End Avenue. His was 401 on 79th Street. We had the same apartment number, 2B. His elevator man always made the same joke that my elevator man made—"2B or not to be." At last, an explanation for why we sometimes got the wrong Chinese-food deliveries.

I guess I gave Jack a pretty good looking-over then. And he looked pretty good. Why should the two people wrapped in blankets have all the fun? Even if one of them had been him? Competition for scarce resources was the way of the world. Survival of the fittest and all that.

I reminded myself that psychological Darwinism was crude.

But still, I thought, Why not? And think how convenient it would be.

At dinner, Jack was already sitting with his family when I came down. He smiled at me, but I had to sit with the Tommasos and Jeremy Toll. Mrs. Tommaso was concerned that the mockingbirds on Tower Island did not get enough water. She proposed bird feeders and birdbaths. Mr. Tommaso said, "My dear, you must let nature take its course," to which Mrs. Tommaso replied, "Well! We know where that leads!"

Jeremy asked me, not for the first time, to tell him about my family's feud.

"I told you," I said. "It's a secret."

"Have I ever told you a secret?" he said.

"No."

He looked at me in an indulgent, meaningful way. "You see?" he said. "You can trust me."

"Of all places," Mrs. Tommaso was saying. "The famous, *world-famous*, Galapagos Islands. Those poor, dear little birds."

I went out to the deck and stood looking over the rail after dinner, hoping Jack would come out, too. But it was Martha who came and stood beside me. She pointed out some unfamiliar constellations. Perhaps she, too, was waiting for someone. For Jack.

"Jack's great," I said.

"Motivated, certainly."

"He lives on my block. He's my neighbor."

"Really? You do get around, Jane."

We stood quietly for a minute. The air was cool and refreshing and oddly soft.

"Now, girls, what's this I hear about a feud?" Jeremy said, appearing suddenly.

"*You're* the gossip columnist," Martha said.

"So I am," Jeremy said with a sigh. He returned to the main cabin.

The wooden deck was smooth and worn. I stared at it awhile, instead of at the stars.

"That poor old feud," I said. "Remember how we used to try to come up with gothic explanations when of course it was all about money?"

"Mmm. Money. It always is."

"And stupid little slights."

"Yes," Martha said. She laughed.

"Sheets!"

"Sheets." She laughed again. "And of course the engagement," she said.

The deck was silent except for the din of the engine, which was a kind of silence itself. Engagement? I hadn't expected Martha to know anything new. It seemed a little ungracious of her.

"Which engagement?" I said. I hoped by phrasing it that way, "Which?" instead of "What?" that I would seem less ignorant, as if I had so many scandalous engagements to choose from.

"Our parents," she said.

Perhaps I stared at her with my mouth open. At any rate, she poked me.

"You didn't know?" she said. "Aunt Anna told me. My father and your mother."

"Were engaged?"

She nodded. "To each other," she added gently, patting my hand.

"So we're idiot sisters? As well as cousins?"

"Your mother broke it off."

Well, I should hope so, I thought.

This new information was bizarre, intriguing, and repellent. Perhaps my father and her mother had been engaged also. Why not? Let the good times roll. I was about to ask Martha how she knew about the broken engagement when Jack came out.

Not now, you fool, I thought. Anyway, which one of us did you come out here to meet?

I had nothing to say to him. I mean, what could I have said? Hey, Jack! Martha just told me that her father and my mother were engaged!

And then he could have replied, Hey, Jane! My father is safely tucked away in a cigar box.

Martha's father had been engaged to my mother. I lay in my little bunk that night, furious that Martha had discovered this fluttering dirty laundry, from my own aunt, who I introduced her to, on her deathbed yet. Martha had come to Barlow, had appropriated my woods by learning all the names of all the trees, and then had appropriated my aunt. As usual I had been kept in the dark. My own mother had not seen fit to enlighten me. I didn't like it that Martha had known something about me that I myself had not known. It wasn't really about me, it was about my mother, but the genetic link was there. And why hadn't Martha told me? What could I have done to have so poisoned her against me? I felt with more certainty than ever the enormity of the deed, whatever it was, however inadvertent. I tried, yet again, to remember what that could have been. Was I sure I had not stolen a boyfriend? Yes, I was sure. That was what I was hoping to do now, perhaps, but I never had in high school. Had some stray scrap of gossip about her, that could have come only from me, reached her ears? But I never gossiped about her, only to her. Perhaps it was the engagement itself that had disenchanted her. She had found out, and then could not bear the sight of me. But I had nothing to do with it. It was before my time. And why, for that matter, *had* my mother broken off the engagement to Martha's father?

"I thought money made the world go round," I said to Gloria.

She grunted in a noncommittal way.

"I thought the feud was about wills."

"Ah! Your family feud!"

"Or incest," I said. "Or at least adultery."

"Yes?" she said. "And?"

"It was about a broken engagement."

Engagements are ridiculous. Animals don't get engaged. They court. The word *engagement* went around and around in my head. We didn't get engaged in college. We hung out or hooked up or moved in together. I wondered what Martha's college years had been like. Or even high school. And then I began to think about high school, that weird island separated from the rest of civilization.

"Okay, Gloria," I said. "Let's look at high school in Darwinian terms for a moment. An isolated geographical area. Once connected to the mainland, but now cut off. You see what I'm getting at? An island. A rugged terrain, few resources. Well, actually, the school had a swimming pool, but I don't mean that. I mean the real food and water of the adolescent, I mean attention and popularity and rebellion and achievement. There's a struggle, right? Every organism for itself. Gradually, over four years, a nanosecond in geological time, but an eternity in teenage time, the organisms appear with slight variations—pants a little baggier, hair a little shorter. Natural selection, high school division, sees this deviation as helpful. It promotes the organism's success in its environment, and so this deviation is encouraged and passed on from grade to grade, and soon more and more exaggerated versions of it spring up —"

"We had to wear uniforms in high school."

"So did we, but you know what I mean."

"I teach high school," Gloria said. "I generally try to view those years as a time of youthful enthusiasm."

"That's what my mother used to say. She's a teacher, too."

"Well, there you are." Gloria smiled at me. "They do outgrow all that, you know."

I tried to think of something I had outgrown since high school, something I could attribute to simple youthful enthusiasm, and it was true that almost all of high school seemed best attributed to youthful enthusiasm. I thought particularly of a teacher I'd had an affair with, a small, potbellied, balding teacher. I didn't really like him. I wasn't attracted to him. It was just a fun, or at least a funnish, thing to do, like driving all night to Boston, then turning around and coming home without getting out of the car. Maybe that was what my mother's engagement to Martha's father had been like. But I had not carried on an extended bitter feud with my English teacher. I couldn't even remember his name.

I lay in bed across from Gloria. She had propped up her pillow by folding a large orange life preserver beneath it. The beam of the bedside light, wan and narrow, groped toward her open book.

I said, "It's condescending to say everyone outgrows everything."

"Yes, you're right. Let me emend my statement: everyone dies. Darwinian enough for you, honey?"

Everybody dies. I had even seen someone die. I had seen the man drown in the swimming pool. Martha and I sat on the side of a grassy hill in our twin bikinis and watched a man drown without even realizing it. I had thought about that day many times. I often wondered if Martha remembered it, too. But she never spoke of it, and the one time I tried to bring it up, a few years later, she told me I was morbid.

"I saw someone die," I said to Gloria. "Martha and I did. It didn't seem real."

I used to reconstruct that day. I would try to determine the exact moment the swimming man became a drowning man. I wrote a story about it for English class when I was in high school. It was the October after the fire. Martha and her family had moved back to New York. In the story, I described Martha's stubby fingers, how they had fascinated me, how they had blotted out the existence of death.

And once again, I remembered that moment when I saw myself as others must have seen me, when I was stunned.

I sent the story to Martha. I had not spoken to her in a couple of weeks. I would not speak to her again for ten years, until I saw her with her sign at the airport on the island of Baltra.

I sent Martha that three-page story typed on my mother's typewriter because it was partly about her, because it was something we'd done, or seen, together, because I thought it would interest her. But perhaps it had not interested her. She probably thought it was morbid. Or just not very good.

I sat on my bunk, and the force of my own embarrassment was sickening. All was revealed—the sin I had committed, the stupid, pipsqueak sin that had extinguished a friendship. I had sent Martha a story about the man drowning at the Barlow Country Club, a story about her fingers, a story about her. She had read the story and never forgiven me.

Maybe she had not liked being observed. Maybe she thought I was poaching, co-opting her life. The story of the drowned man and the stubby fingers had disgusted Martha, angered her. Martha thought I had betrayed her, betrayed a confidence. Or she was simply insulted because I noticed, and remembered, and reported on her short fat fingers.

Martha's fingers were still a little stubby.

But, really, Martha, I thought, it wasn't just your story. It was mine too.

That whole night and the next morning, I argued mentally with Martha:

It was just a story. Couldn't she tell the difference between a character in a story and a real person?

It was all true. I didn't make anything up, so how could she object to my describing what really happened?

It was a sign of loyalty that I had written about something that happened to us so long ago, and a sign of loyalty that I had sent it to her to see.

It had absolutely nothing to do with her. It was just an English assignment. Why make such a federal case out of it?

I sent it to her, so obviously I had nothing to hide.

Why should I have told her anything, anyway? She never told me about our parents' being engaged.

————⁓⁓⁓————

I continued this dialogue the next morning. I walked in my thinking circles thinking about Martha and my mother and her father and her dwarf fingers. And then there she was before me, sitting on a deck chair with a notebook open on her lap. I sat down on the chair next to her.

"Today we'll see daisies that have evolved into trees," she said. She closed the notebook. I tried not to stare at her stumpy fingers. She pulled a guidebook from under the chair. She pointed to a picture of a spiky bush crowned by stunted daisies.

Your fingers aren't that bad, I thought. Why are you so sensitive about them?

"See?" she was saying. "Daisy trees. A forest of them. They won't be in bloom, though."

"Are you sure about the engagement?"

"Aunt Anna told me in the hospital, right before she died. She wouldn't tell me why they split up, though."

"I wonder why she didn't tell me."

"I don't know why she *did* tell me. She was probably having nicotine withdrawal. And she really did give me those pearls, after all. She was amazing, your Aunt Anna."

"Why didn't you tell me?"

Martha looked up from her book. She was chewing gum. She shrugged.

"I don't know. I never saw you. I just did tell you."

———✦———

And then at last we boarded the *pangas* for the island of Floreana.

"*Don't* leave Grandpa here," Dot said when Martha and Gloria began chatting about the Ritters, the Wittmers, the baroness, and the corpses.

Jack put his arm around Dot and kissed her head, just the way my mother used to kiss mine. Martha looked at them curiously, and I thought, first, that Martha did not know about the deceased William Cornwall coming on the trip, and, second, that William Cornwall really had come on the trip. Grandpa was a stowaway in an urn. Take nothing but pictures. Leave nothing but Grandpa.

"They ought to be ashamed of themselves," Mrs. Tommaso said.

"Who?" I said. Did she mean the Cornwalls? Would she tell Martha, who might then be obligated to confiscate Mr. Cornwall?

"The human race."

"Oh, them," Gloria said.

Craig and Cindy were holding hands, and I wondered if they had been inspired and touched by the story of the Ritters. Perhaps every couple, when they get married and decide to have children, think they are somehow starting a new line. A new line. Like dresses with shorter skirts for the spring. Pantsuits this fall, sleeker, more feminine, in the new synthetics! Lineage *is* a little like fashion. A closet full of DNA. Natural selection has to go out unexpectedly tonight! The weather is terrible, a goddamn flood. She'll ruin her shoes! What will she wear? Paws? Claws? No, no, those fabulous sunflower-yellow web feet!

We spent the morning at a beach that was made of green sand. Martha told us about the olivine crystals in the volcanic tuff. She held out a handful of the dark, sparkling sand, and I looked at it through the wrong end of my binoculars. I could see the dainty crystals, smooth and egg-shaped, resting on Martha's outstretched palm.

Darwin sailed to the Galapagos to find the answer to the mystery of mysteries. I had sailed to the Galapagos, I had come all this way, and what had I found?

One: Martha hated me because of something in that English story. That explanation seemed more and more plausible, if only because of the timing involved. I sent it to her. I never heard from her again. Q.E.D.

Two: My mother was once engaged to her own cousin. He probably wanted to go sailing with her, so she had to break up with him. A splitting event. Then she met my father. He said, "I don't sail. I row. But only in college." And she had fallen gratefully into his arms. Their passion flourished, landlocked. I felt, I had always felt, that my parents belonged together in some very profound way. I wondered if that belief in their fitness for each other made my marriage to Michael more precarious. My parents seemed destined for each other. I had never felt destined for Michael. I did not feel destined, period. But then, if all of creation was the fallout from various happy accidents, perhaps I didn't have to be destined, only opportunistic. I tried to think of Jack as my new niche.

We sat on the beach and watched Cindy play with the hermit

crabs she found on the mangrove roots. I wanted to ask Martha more about the engagement. How old were they? How had they met? I tried to imagine them making love, or even kissing, their identical blue eyes staring like incestuous mirrors.

I wondered again if Craig could have been one of the wandering nocturnal blankets, or the man talking to the woman outside my window a few days before. I listened carefully to his mild voice as he asked Jack if he was satisfied with his hiking shoes. And what *about* Jack? Perhaps if I knocked on Jack's cabin door later, he would say, "Is that you?" like the anonymous blankets, and I would recognize the voice. How could I get him to say, "But where? When? Oh, if only . . ." like the man outside the cabin window?

Silly thing to think about as one sits on a green beach viewing the biological mysteries. Silly to think about assignations or English papers from long ago or broken engagements. I felt vaguely guilty, petty. And yet we were on Floreana, isle of the guilty, isle of the petty, an island even a naturephobe could love, a soap opera of an island, a great seething volcanic cauldron of human vanity, a land of no opportunity, and even that squandered. Floreana, the New Jersey of the Galapagos. Pirates and fierce red-haired hermits, a penal colony, and, best of all: The Nietzschean Dentist and His Lame Love Slave! The Austrian Whip-Cracking Faux Baroness—Self-Proclaimed Galapagos Empress!—and Her Three Abject Lovers! Jacob Astor's Yacht! Nudists! Norwegians!

"If flies and horses and humans all evolved separately," said Jack's sister, Liza, "along different branches of the universal tree of life, how did we all get eyes?"

Our cameras and binoculars hung like huge beads from our scarlet necks.

"Eyes are useful," Martha said after a while.

Frau Wittmer received us in the dining room of her post

office–hotel. She stood in a cotton housedress beneath maps of Germany and a print of the cathedral at Cologne. Dark wooden beams, lace curtains, and flowered tablecloths—we could have been in the Black Forest with Hansel and Gretel. We were in a fable, a German fable transported to a Pacific island. The white-haired, pink-cheeked suspected murderess with sparkling blue eyes shook hands and posed for photographs. Even Mrs. Cornwall recognized that here was a matriarch of unusual stature. Over the years, Margret Wittmer's name had come up in connection with seven murders. She outlived the superman dentist by many decades. Some people think she killed him, for he died after eating a portion of that potted chicken she sent around each month. I don't blame her for that one, though. Ritter was a vegetarian, and he had some scientific training. He ought to have known that chicken is not a vegetable. And when he fed it to his livestock, the stuff had killed them. Most of us, even without that training in dentistry, would at this point throw the potted chicken away. But perhaps because Herr Doktor Ritter was more than a dentist, because he was a philosopher, he boiled the spoiled potted meat. Then he ate it. Then he died. I'm sorry, I don't think you can lay that one at the feet of old Margret.

When I saw Margret Wittmer, so pink and white and robust, I wanted only to marvel at her as I had at the frigate birds with their inflated red balloon necks, at all the flora and fauna, at the volcanoes on which they all lived. As Gloria raised her camera to take a picture of me with Frau Wittmer, the old lady quickly pulled her glasses off, then stared blankly in the direction of the camera lens and smiled. She seemed to me in that instant so utterly human and so absurdly vain. It was unnerving.

Behind her house, or, properly, her hotel, there was a pen in which she raised Galapagos tortoises. They sunned themselves, hardly distinguishable from the dirt of the little corral. We walked past them, down the dusty road that ran by the few other houses, in which lived various Wittmer descendants. Chickens scratched at the dust. Martha pointed out some trees. I heard someone behind me grumbling that this excursion had nothing to do with natural history.

Jack, who was walking quietly beside me, said, "Quite the contrary."

Jack's face was golden in the equatorial sun. I walked beside this friendly man with beautiful eyes, and I thought, Perhaps my same old self, which I've accidentally brought along to this new world, will get to work in a brand-new way, will blossom and flower, like a thick-trunked tree of daisies.

"It may be argued [that] representative species [are] chiefly found where [there are] barriers," Darwin wrote in an entry in one of his notebooks, "and what are barriers but [an] interruption of communication?"

Gloria pointed this passage out to me after lunch. She said she felt as if there had been an interruption of communication. I thought she meant communication with me, and I agreed, saying perhaps she should listen more carefully when I told her my interesting theories about high school and such, but it turned out she meant that she felt far, far away, just as I did, just as Jack did, just as we all did.

"Look! Here's a definition of species for you," she said, pointing to a passage in the huge red paperback volume of Darwin's notebooks. She was looking through it as we stretched out on our bunks for a short siesta.

"Definition of species: one that remains at large with constant characters, together with other beings of very near structure—

Hence species may be good ones and differ scarcely in any external character:—For instance two wrens forced to haunt two islands one with one kind of herbage and one with other, might change organization of stomach and hence remain distinct."

"But how near is 'very near structure'?" I said. "At what point do we say 'Aha! Not near enough'?"

"You'll have to find that one yourself," Gloria said. She tossed the book onto my bed.

"I think the organization of my stomach has changed," I said. I felt vaguely seasick and I took a nap. When I woke up, Gloria was gone. A gloomy peace suffused the cabin. I lay in the stillness listening to the boat's creaks and nautical groans. And then I heard the voices, the same voices. They were rendezvousing in the same place, criminals returned to the scene of their crime.

"Can we ever make this work?" said the man softly.

"Of course we will," said the woman. "Soon."

"You can't imagine what it's like," he said. "Every day. Having to pretend . . ."

"I know it's hard."

"Thank you," he said. "Thank you."

It was Jack. It was Martha. I heard them clearly this time. I recognized their voices. I tried to determine if I was dreaming. I often have lifelike banal dreams about someone calling and canceling an appointment or complaining about an unpaid bill, which I have a difficult time identifying as dreams in the morning. But this dream hardly qualified as ordinary. Perhaps the changed organization of my stomach had produced a changed organization of my dreams. That was a more welcome explanation than Jack and Martha making assignations outside my window.

We landed on a small beach on another part of Floreana late in the afternoon and walked a few hundred yards on a path toward the interior. I watched the vegetation change as we crossed from the coastal zone to the arid zone. The change was ridiculously abrupt, as if the plants knew where they belonged, which I suppose they did, in a way.

I was more angry than I'd been in a long time. Of course things changed. I understood that. Things change. Things change in time. The Galapagos Islands had changed from hot, sterile, volcanic explosions into oases of oddball populations. Things change in space. Even in that short distance, we were moving from one ecological environment to another. Things die. I understood that, too. Who didn't? Things happen for no reason. Yes, yes, the commonplaces of modern life. Bumper stickers. I got it.

Still, one was not a Buddha. One was a human being, flesh and blood and nerve endings and chemical messages to one's brain. And those messages said, "Fuck you, Martha."

We arrived at a small clearing. In the middle was the post-office barrel atop a heap of sticks and boards and flags, like a big wooden bird on a big wooden nest. There were plaques and carved medallions from visiting groups like ours, laminated ID tags from students, and one or two religious medals.

The post-office barrel, or one like it, had been on that spot for over a hundred years. Sailors, whalers mostly, on outgoing trips would leave letters for ships on their way home and vice versa. My great-great-grandfather might have mailed a letter here. Now tourists left letters. If I, for example, had found a letter addressed to someone in New York City, I would have taken that letter home and delivered it or put a local stamp on it and popped it in a normal blue mailbox.

Martha removed a plastic bag full of letters from the barrel and began looking at the addresses. Many from Germany. Many from Israel. France. England. Ohio. There were also about two dozen business cards from lawyers.

Fuck you, Martha, I thought.

We sat down and milled around and read other people's postcards. Jeremy Toll seemed the most animated of the group. The light grew dimmer, but if you squinted you could still eavesdrop on these unknown correspondents. "Wish you were here!" the postcards said in one language or another. "Hope you get this!"

"They're all writing to their children," Jeremy said. "How utterly unimaginative."

I had a postcard I'd bought earlier that day from Margret Wittmer's hotel. I addressed it to my mother and father. It said, "Thank you. Love, Jane."

"What lovely manners," Jeremy said, looking over my shoulder.

It was dusk. The sky was a beautiful dark softening blue. Gloria was staring off in a particularly distracted way.

"What's a species?" I said.

"Oh, Jane."

"Darwin saw that every barnacle was different from every other barnacle, right? So how can they all be barnacles? If every one is different?"

Gloria said she was sorry the trip was almost over. "It's very beautiful here in a stark and impersonal way."

I looked out at the bushes around us, at the sky, which had turned the color of iron. It was getting cold. Fuck you, Martha, I thought again. And then again.

"It's ironic, isn't it," Gloria said, "that the scientific understanding that led us to realize that we are one with the animal kingdom relied on the recognition of the existence of the individual."

Brian and Liza Cornwall and Mrs. Cornwall herself squatted on the sand to read the notes, the ID tags, the wooden plaques left hanging from the post-office barrel as souvenirs, great heaps of sentimental trash. The Tommasos were scrutinizing a stalk. Craig and Cindy flipped through the lawyers' business cards for familiar names. Jeannie sat with Ethel, Jeremy sat with Dot.

Gloria pointed to the group. "A species is a collection of individuals," she said.

But I didn't say anything, for I realized that two individuals were missing from the collection. Martha and Jack.

"The individuals have certain things in common," Gloria went on. "Historically those things have changed. Aristotle grouped animals differently than we do today. People have used all kinds of criteria—what animals ate, whether or not we eat them, or how many legs they had, or whether they had fur or feathers. Now we look at populations that can share DNA. Okay? Does that help? Species are real, with real boundaries, but they're always changing. All right? They're statistical entities. You're part of a species, but you're still you. And you can't mate with a barnacle."

"Just sheep," Jeremy called from the log where he was sitting.

"That's called a sheep shagger," Dot said.

"You astonish me, young lady," said Jeremy. "And delight me."

Gloria gave me a fairly friendly push, then turned away to resume contemplating the sky, which was now even deeper and darker. It was the latest we had ever been ashore anywhere.

"Where's Martha?" I said.

"She went up that path," Jeannie said. "Some old ruin of a cement mixer or something equally fascinating. I prefer other people's mail."

If Martha had wandered off, I could wander off after her. The ruin of a cement mixer sounded important and intellectually engaging. I could ask her more about the relationship of the individual to the species. I could ask her more about our parents' broken engagement. What could I ask Jack about? Well, it wasn't as if I were following them. Fuck them.

I slipped away from the group and walked nonchalantly along the path that Jeannie had pointed out. It was almost dark, and I reminded myself that the only wild animals on this island were mice and cows and donkeys and cats and dogs. Strays. Brought there on ships, left behind by ships. Goats. Rats. It was quiet. So different from Barlow at dusk with all its birds and squirrels and insects. So different from New York, where people called for taxis and discussed their therapists and fought with invisible spouses on cell phones. I looked through the gloom at the barren landscape.

"Taxi!" I said, very softly.

I spent only a few minutes sneaking, lonely, through the scant brush. Then I saw them.

They stood close to each other.

"This is perfect," Jack said.

"I told you it would be worth the wait," Martha said.

Jack put his arms around Martha.

"You're incredible," he said.

"Just one of the Ecuadorian park ranger's many services," she said.

"Taxi!" I said, as Martha caught sight of me.

I think you could say they both blanched. They moved away from each other. Jack muttered, "Oh dear." Martha coughed.

"Hi!" I said.

"Hi," they answered.

"I was just . . ." I started to say. But I was just what? Following them? That didn't sound very nice. "I'm really sorry. I didn't mean to —"

But I did mean. I meant to follow them, to find them and, I realized, I meant to tell Martha off, finally, after all these years.

"I'm sorry I didn't mention this before," Jack said. He walked over and took my hand.

I took my hand back. I was here to see Martha, to speak to Martha, to confront Martha. I would deal with him later. Or not. He was a sidebar. I moved past him. I faced Martha.

"We have to get a few things straight, Martha."

"I know it's not right," Jack said, "but —"

"I'm not even talking to you," I said.

"Yes, I know, but —"

"I don't care if it's right. What does that mean, anyway? I'm not interested. I have to talk to *Martha*. Martha has to talk to me. There are too many stupid secrets and misunderstandings."

"I know it's awful to keep it secret, but it was important," Martha said. She smiled, which I thought almost indecent under the circumstances.

"Martha had to keep this a secret. She could get into trouble," Jack said. "She's been so wonderful. She figured out the logistics, she made this possible, she found the perfect place. She had to keep this a secret, you can understand that."

"Wrong secret," I said.

"Well, all secrets are wrong," Jack said.

"No, they're not," Martha said. "That's not true."

The two of them began earnestly debating when it was morally permissible to keep information from someone else. Jack felt that if the information would hurt the other person, you could keep it to yourself and remain in the clear ethically if not morally.

"If you see what I mean."

While Martha believed that silence and discretion could in and of themselves be a form of moral courage.

"You agree with me, don't you, Jane?" she said. "Now, let's proceed with the business at hand."

Jack smiled. "Yes," he said. "At last."

Okay, okay, uncle! I give up! How could I properly confront Martha now, as she prepared her woodland bower of lust, like Dido drawing Aeneas to her love cave? Proceed with your epic lovemaking. Go about your business. Just stop talking. Stop these hideous confidences.

I turned to go back.

"Oh, you can stay," Jack said.

"You can watch," Martha said. "Quietly."

This is what you get for stalking people, Jane, I thought. Seek and ye shall find.

"Mom should be here any minute," Jack said.

"She should?"

"This is all for her, really."

"It is?"

"But my sister and the rest of the gang are coming, too. Quite an event, isn't it?"

"You're a very close-knit family."

He put his arm around Martha's shoulders.

"Don't be nervous," she said.

"So we're like going native?" I said.

"There are no natives here," Martha said. "Unless you count Margret Wittmer."

"I know this seems silly, Jane, but people need rituals."

The rest of the voyeurs arrived and stood in a circle around Martha and Jack, and I saw that this was probably not a mating ceremony, but a marriage ceremony.

"I think we should hold hands," Mrs. Cornwall said.

Only Dot seemed embarrassed.

"Now we'll sing," Mrs. Cornwall said.

Then they all seemed embarrassed. But they sang. "Swing Low, Sweet Chariot."

Jack walked over to me, and whispered, "Cheer up."

Then Mrs. Cornwall whipped out a cardboard box from her backpack. She opened it and sprinkled Mr. Cornwall on the ground.

"Maybe I should keep a little," she said. "I've grown accustomed to —"

"To what?" Jack said. "His weight? Come on, Mother. Enough is enough."

"Now's the time," said Jack's sister, more gently.

"This is gross," said Dot.

We walked back along the path in a pure and utter darkness. So, I thought, natural selection is a kind of cosmic farce, in which it all comes out right in the end because whatever comes out in the end is by definition right because there is no right and wrong?

Maybe Martha was correct. Maybe metaphor was a mistake.

11

T HE FRIGHTENING THING about Darwin is not nature red in tooth and claw. The frightening thing about Darwin is not our ancestors the apes. The frightening thing about Darwin is what my mother called chaos. I realize that there is some specific scientific meaning to the word *chaos*. But I think that my mother's meaning is more profound: there is no plan, there never was one. Everyone knows this. It is a cliché of modernism. Everyone knows this now. But Darwin knew it first. And Darwin knew it best. Darwin met chaos head on. He saw it wandering aimlessly, meaninglessly, shifting and turning without warning through a world in which every creature considered itself the most important and not one of them mattered a whit. My mother found this notion to be invigorating, and maybe it is. But imagine realizing it for the first time, realizing it not just personally, but on behalf of the entire Western world. For the years after his great journey, after his discovery of the mechanism of the randomness of our existence, after his discovery of chaos, Darwin suffered mysterious illnesses—long bouts of diarrhea, vomiting, blinding headaches, fainting spells, weakness, and exhaustion. It might have been some virus he picked up on his travels. He may have been allergic to the chemicals he used to preserve specimens. And it may have been psychosomatic, a physical revulsion at the truth he had discovered. And yet, picture this: It is a spring morning. Darwin has been home from his *Beagle* adventure for years. He stands in his garden, waiting, armed with a flour sifter borrowed from the kitchen. A bee lands on the rose in front of him. Darwin dusts it with a fine white coating of flour. He alerts his assistants—little Darwin girls in their pinafores and little Darwin boys in their short pants, the Darwin governess in her sweeping skirts, all posted at strategic points surrounding the garden. Charles Darwin is wearing a frock coat. They run after the dusty white bee, following its path. The path of the bee, even in the midst of a world of meaninglessness, means something to Darwin. And Darwin, a bearded Victorian paterfamilias, running through his glorious flower garden chasing a bee with his children and their governess—that means something, too.

Looking for the dolphins that never materialized one morning, I told Gloria I had read about Darwin's powdered bee in one of her books.

"Imagine him, thinking up some way to mark the bee, chasing it all over with his kids, with the nanny. Pocket watch banging against his belly. Now, that's what I call science."

Martha, walking by us as I was talking, said, "Poor bee."

This made me want to kill her. Perhaps it is not nature but friendship that is red in tooth and claw. Perhaps a family feud or even a personal feud with my best friend, Martha, should never have come as a surprise to me. Perhaps the feud is the paradigm of all relationships, a long history of exaggerated slights, of misinterpreted actions and misguided reactions. Neo-Darwinists have said that natural selection is an algorithmic process, an unthinking, unchanging equation that governs all of life, all of creation. What if they're wrong? What if it's the feud that regulates life? Feuds are algorithmic, unthinking, unchanging. No matter what you plug into them, the answer is the same. At that moment, I think I liked the idea of feuding with the entire universe. It made me feel connected.

Darwin lived with the secret of creation tearing at his conscience and his intestines for twenty years. Some historians think he was cowardly for not announcing his theory much earlier. Others think he was, rather, a responsible, meticulous scientist. Secrets are funny things, leading a potential existence, an actual existence, a virtual existence, a nonexistence. Secrets don't make any more sense than feuds do.

The Cornwalls' secret was safe with me, that I knew. But not because I felt any protective need to guard it, or by extension, them. It was safe with me because, like so many secrets, once it was revealed to me, it lost its interest, its power. And it embarrassed me. My role in it, as an eager supplicant stalking the cool and distant Martha, embarrassed me. Jack's role embarrassed me, too. Poor Jack, traveling all that way to sing around the campfire of Dad's ashes. The whole Cornwall family, Mr. Cornwall in particular, all embarrassed me. Only Dot, so embarrassed herself, seemed unscathed by the absurd event on Floreana Island.

The next morning, when we set off for our island du jour, a flat rock called South Plaza, I pushed Floreana from my head and placed Gloria's hat (a vast straw object she had purchased at the airport in Guayaquil "for an emergency") on it instead. I was the emergency, for in spite of ginger pills and Dramamine and

acupressure bands on my wrists, I was still suffering from seasickness.

"Maybe the absence of meaning in the world has distressed your
stomach," Gloria said. "As it did Darwin's."

"Maybe."

The hat flopped lightly on all sides, blocking my vision, but reassuring me. The sky was gray, but painfully bright and hot. Floreana with its macabre hillbilly feuds, with its murders and mum-
mies and, now, the ashes of Mr. William Cornwall, was left far
behind.

Mrs. Cornwall did seem a little down in the mouth, though.

"Separation anxiety," Jack whispered to me, nodding at his glum
mother. He seemed a bit forlorn himself.

I made a polite response of assent, a murmur sort of thing. We
had seemed to have an understanding, Jack and I, if only for a moment, a subtle, sub-rosa protoflirtation that might not have been a
flirtation at all—that kind of understanding. But, Really, I thought,
you have made me very uncomfortable with your dance of death.

"I'm bored," Dot said. "I'm hot. I want a real shower."

"Decadent creature," said Jeremy.

I avoided Martha, as much as one can avoid the leader of a
group. I hung back, drifted ahead, sat off to the side on a rock—
anything to steer clear of Martha's stories, Martha's voice. She certainly didn't notice. She talked, on and on.

We walked through a forest of dry, white trees called Palo Santo
trees from which another species of booby, with French blue beaks
and tomato red–webbed feet, watched us from their nests. Little
bundles of white down wriggled beneath them, occasionally poking a beak up, demanding to be fed. Sometimes a male blue-
footed booby would whistle at us on the narrow trail and peck at

our legs. I used Gloria's hat as a shield, holding it against my leg each time we passed a whistling booby glaring at us with those round, close-set booby eyes. Then we made our way across a rocky plateau spattered with white guano paint. Swallow-tailed gulls swept fearlessly from the sky to their nests deep in the cliffs. We posed for pictures beneath towering cactus trees. The heat accompanied us everywhere.

The blue-footed birds hissed at us as we passed out of the grove of bare trees to be greeted by a vast rocky plateau dotted with their circular nests, nests that were nothing but white lime rings, orbits of guano sprayed on the inhospitable rocks, circles of shit.

"Circle of death," Jack reminded us, dutifully, without his usual zeal.

Jack was shimmering. Why was he shimmering?

The boobies sat on the ground surrounded by their bull's-eyes of guano. We stood, staring at the circles of shit, silent and intent.

The boobies were shimmering. Martha was shimmering. Gloria was shimmering, too, beside a shimmering Cindy. Why was everyone shimmering? Was it from the heat? Interesting that everyone was shimmering. I closed my eyes for a moment, but that only made the swaying and shimmering worse.

I looked at the white circles. Inside was caked brown dust. Outside was caked brown dust. Inside was home. Outside was death.

"Shocking," said Mrs. Tommaso.

"Gloria thinks anthropomorphism can cloud your understanding," I said.

"Or clarify it!" said Gloria. She turned to one of the birds, squatted down beside it, and looked it right in its close-set booby eyes. "Isn't that right, dear?" she said.

South Plaza was the location, among other things, of a bachelor colony of sea lions. They all hung out here, the hapless males who couldn't score. Martha made some jokes about their lack of housekeeping, which I thought were rather lame until we approached the colony and the smell of sea lion excrement and urine greeted us, as thick as a curtain.

I followed Gloria along the narrow trail. She still shimmered and swayed in the heat, like an oasis. I stopped to catch my breath. The sun had come out, burning off the mist, and the heat was becoming even more oppressive.

Martha was talking. I noticed from a great distance. I was standing right beside Martha, but the heat blurred her words. I sensed that she was relating a crucial chapter in her big book of nature, but I could not take in the words.

The bachelors sprawled on the rocks. Some of them had come here to recuperate after a frenzy of copulating and fighting and keeping the harem in line. Some were waiting to go out and overthrow some equally exhausted bull. Some were losers who would never get a girl, much less a harem. They looked fat to me—gross, wallowing, snoring, grunting. They weren't cute at all. How could I ever have thought such a thing? They were stinking slovenly males. They probably didn't even lift the seat when they peed. They left their used tissues on the kitchen table. They didn't put the milk back in the fridge.

I put one foot in front of the other, then brought the first foot forward, then repeated, one foot, then the other foot, stepping forever over sharp hunks of lava. Pahoehoe lava? Or the other kind? What was the other kind called? If only the lava and the stinking sea lion piss would disappear. If only the boat would appear. A porter in a white sailor suit would pull back the covers on the narrow cot in the cool, dark cabin, and I would put this swaying, whirling body down to rest.

"Someone said that poetry was a product of the lower intestines," Jeremy said. "And I should like to say that I feel this place is truly poetic."

"Do you want some water?" Gloria asked me.

I think I moved my hand in a gesture that suggested, No, thank you.

She snapped my picture. "You're actually green."

I sat on a rock. It was not green, it was white, white with bird shit. But a pool of greenish sea lion urine lay just beyond my left foot. I heard Martha's voice as she lectured nearby, the inflection familiar and comforting.

I stood up. I tugged off the vast straw hat. The cord was around my neck, caught in the cord of my binoculars, the cord of my camera, the cord of my sunglasses. I tugged at all the cords. Martha's voice stopped talking. I felt hands helping me. Fingers pulled the cords apart, like the fingers of a nineteenth-century gentleman unlacing a lady about to faint. My father once told me men used to carry little scissors with them so they could unsnip the corset laces quickly. Was someone unsnipping my binocular cords with a Swiss Army knife? I wondered this as I vomited violently onto the hallowed ground of Darwin's Galapagos Islands. I wondered this briefly, then realized it was not true as I noticed that I was not only vomiting violently, tearing my throat in great heaving rasps, but was also fiercely emitting something warm into my special quick-dry nylon underpants, something I first thought was urine, then knew was not.

I straightened up. A moment of calm. I remembered a poem my grandma Schwartz had taught me:

Holy Moses, king of the Jews,
Pissed in his britches
And shat in his shoes.

I turned my head. I saw Martha. The feud had come to this. I was unfit.

But then Martha handed me a Kleenex. She handed me a plastic bag. She held out a plastic box of some kind of wipes, the kind you use for babies. How prescient. She gave me a handful. She grabbed some more and began mopping at my legs.

I looked down at the mess and thought, Wouldn't it be nice if Mrs. Cornwall had waited or kept a handful of Mr. Cornwall in reserve and could dump her husband right here, where he could do some good, soak up the spill, like sawdust in the butcher shop.

Martha stood with me while I repeated my performance. Martha stood with me while I dabbed at my legs, at my boots. She produced more and more paper products. She squeezed her water bottle at me, washing off some of the worst mess. She wiped me up with the tender indifference of a mother cleaning a baby's bottom. She sealed the Ziploc bag, then another and another. She carried the hat and the camera and the binoculars. She took out the shirt I had in my backpack and tied it around my waist. It occurred to me that I ought to be embarrassed, humiliated, mortified, shamed. I thought for a moment of the nuances of meaning that separated those words, but realized I felt none of them, I felt only gratitude. I must have been wrong about the Barlow family feud. There was no family feud anymore, no genetic legacy of discord, no primogeniture, no Romeo and Juliet.

Most of the others had already gone in the first *panga* when we got back to this island's set of concrete steps with this island's sleeping seal. I thanked God, who did not exist and whose fault this whole thing was, that Jack was among them, and my girlish pride seemed quaint to me, even at the time. I sat down in the *panga* and tried not to think about what I was sitting in. I wondered if I might not have some prevocal memory of being a baby, but I didn't. In that moment of extreme vulnerability, sitting in my own shit, I actually felt almost happy. I had been reduced to a Job-like state of low humiliation and filth, of powerless pathos, and no one minded! I was nothing, less than nothing. All was vanity. And Martha had cleaned me off with the best will in the world.

A great responsibility had been lifted from my shoulders.

"Shame is a kind of narcissism," I said. But perhaps I did not say it out loud. No one would have heard me, anyway, over the roar of the outboard motor.

Ethel and Jeannie were with us, I think. I know Gloria was there, because she took off her own sweatshirt (which, she had informed me that morning, was knit out of fibers from old Coke bottles) and without a word laid it across my knees in a delicate offering. I knew it would be invaluable when I stood up, but I couldn't bear to defile this holy garment, this token of generosity toward me in my moment of need, this symbol of self-sacrifice and spiritual greatness.

Gloria was a goddess. No, Jane, for once, just say, Gloria is a wonderful human being. Human beings can be this wonderful. They don't have to be goddesses. Just look at Martha. Could this really be the same person who had made my life not miserable exactly, but *narrower*, who had left me high and dry, deserted, an island of narcissistic confusion, because of some story written ten years ago? No, probably it could not be the same person. This Martha was very real, her backpack full of soiled wipes in little

Ziploc bags. So what, then, was the other Martha? Just an idea in my head? I really didn't know.

I had no idea! How odd. I always had ideas, didn't I, a sandstorm of ideas, of theories and metaphors. No, not a sandstorm. It was more like a disease, like Tourette's syndrome, an uncontrollable barking. I was compulsively metaphorical, a victim of echolalia, repeating every one of the earth's utterances.

When we were in high school, Martha said something to me that I had never understood and until that moment, sitting in shit on a dinghy in the Pacific Ocean, I had never thought of again. But now I remembered it.

She said, "You're so self-centered. But you're not introspective. No offense."

"I am not self-centered. And I think about myself *all the time*."

Martha had laughed. I asked her what book she had just finished reading and said I was sure she was just thinking about some character in it rather than me because she didn't have an original idea in her head, and she had sighed in a way that made me think I'd won the little argument.

But then she said, "You have a hypothesis about everything but yourself."

I tried to fend off the crew member who wanted to help me untie my bootlaces when we boarded the *Huxley*. I tried not to drip as Martha and Gloria helped me make my way up the little stairway to the cabin. I think I said thank you. I think I said it over and over again. Then, at my cabin door, Martha turned to go.

"I left more than footsteps," I said.

"You know, I make jewelry out of pigeon shit," Gloria said. "You dry the pellets in the microwave, and then polish them in one of those rock tumblers."

"You've altered evolution," Martha said.

"Thank you," Gloria said.

"Not you," Martha said. "*Jane*. You've altered evolution. Now you can rest after your labors."

I showered in my clothes. I threw the quick-dry underwear and the socks in the garbage with the toilet paper. I washed the rest in shampoo, then Woolite. Gloria, who had waited anxiously in the cabin, offered to take the wet shirt and shorts up top and hang them to dry, but I felt suddenly too shy to give her so intimate an assignment. I took them myself and climbed unsteadily up the ladder, hung the dripping clothes on the line, halfheartedly pushed a clothespin in their general direction, and stumbled down again, nearly swooning as I collapsed on my bunk.

Gloria was gone, but she reappeared soon after with a cup of exotic, delicious tea and some dry toast.

"Eduardo the cook thought you might want this," she said.

"What is this wonderful tea?" I said. "It's so soothing. Maybe it's marijuana. Or Ecuadorian rain-forest bark."

"Jane, it's chamomile."

The breeze came in through the windows, rattling the blinds. I drank the tea. I ate one piece of toast. The engines roared. I wondered how Gloria knew the cook's name and I didn't. I wondered at the weird way in which one sometimes doesn't see what's in front of one, in which I did not see what was in front of me, like chamomile. Sometimes. The *Huxley* set off for a new island. I slept.

I woke up now and then, looked around me, sipped cold chamomile tea. I thought about Martha a little. As I rested in a cloud of enervated nausea, I thought of the feud, thought there were worse things than broken engagements, or even broken friendships, for I was overwhelmed again by that one feeling—

gratitude. I lay in my bunk, my body limp and weak, and slept through the afternoon field trip, a visit to an island called Santa Fe. When she came back, Gloria said there were huge land iguanas there and cacti as big as trees.

"You can have copies of my pictures," Gloria said, aiming her camera at my sickly face. I blinked at the flash in the darkened room.

"Especially that one," I said.

When she came out of the bathroom after her shower, she stood before me, toothbrush in hand, hair flying in all directions, wearing a T-shirt decorated with a design of small irregular white blobs meant to resemble bird shit, each one labeled with the name of a different species.

"Martha is an ideal guide, isn't she?" Gloria said. "I can see how it must have been a challenge to be friends with her."

I was so grateful to Gloria that every time I looked at her I wanted to reach out and pet her. This wave of good fellowship I felt for her had previously affected me only with regard to cats and dogs. Who's a good Gloria? Who loves her Gloria? Who's the best Gloria in the whole wide world? But I resented her saying anything about Martha. My stomach rested delicately, a neurasthenic inmate just quieted down, a hysteric who could not be disturbed in any manner.

"Martha held my head when I vomited. She gave me wet wipes," I said. "And you gave me your sweatshirt. All of evolution, all of civilization, marched in teleological progression toward that glorious moment."

Gloria pulled off the bird-shit classification T-shirt and put on another with a picture of pathetic baby seals. I looked at Gloria, my savior, my nurse, and veered between wanting to pet her and wanting to club her baby seals.

"Martha has forgiven me," I said. "For whatever it was I said or did, she reached down, like an athlete at the end of his endurance, and found that little something extra. She reached down deep inside and forgave me. I guess."

Gloria felt my head, gave me a motherly kiss, and shook her own head, slightly, ruefully, as if at my sad attempts to flap my poor little residual organ.

"Or did I forgive her? Anyway, the feud is over."

"You better take some more Tylenol," Gloria said. "You're burning up."

Martha walked by, looked in, knocked on the air of the open door.

"Come in," Gloria said. "The patient is all tucked up, ready to weather the stormy weather."

"Are you feeling any better?"

Martha sat on the edge of the bunk, her body pulling the tight covers even tighter. I felt like a mummy. Her hip was jutting into my ribs. It was difficult to breathe.

"There, there," she said.

At least she didn't say, "There, now."

Her eyes glanced around the little cabin.

"Good. Everything is shipshape in here." She looked back at me. "Even you." I was forgiven, absolved, pardoned, exonerated. Go with God, go in peace, go forth and multiply. Her magnanimity flowethed over.

"My story was so harmless," I said. I hadn't meant to say anything. But sometimes even conversation is opportunistic.

"What story?" Martha said.

"I'm sorry I wrote it if it offended you. Well, it obviously did offend you, but I didn't mean anything by it. And how could it offend you? You said much worse things about me. And vice versa. I thought you'd be interested. You're always so interested in every-thing."

"She's delirious," Gloria said. "Jane! Can you hear me? I am Gloria, your roommate."

"I never even found out what that man's name was. He died right in front of us, he drowned right in front of our eyes and we never even asked who he was," I said.

"Maybe you shouldn't be tucked in quite so tight," Gloria was saying.

"Jane, calm down," Martha said. "No one is dead. No one drowned. Everyone is fine."

"Why didn't you tell me the story made you so angry? Why did it make you angry, anyway? I sent you an innocent English paper, and you never spoke to me again! Why couldn't you just tell me what the problem was?"

Martha looked alarmed now.

"There is no problem," she said in a soothing voice.

"Maybe it wasn't chamomile tea," Gloria said.

"I'm not delirious," I said. I tried to sit up in the tight blankets, but they were held down by Martha sitting close beside me. I struggled inside of them. "I'm not delirious!"

"Jane, Jane, it's okay. No one drowned. It was a lovely snorkel."

I finally loosened the blankets from the other side of the bunk and sat up. "Look," I said. "The man died. The man at the Barlow Country Club. Remember?"

"No," Martha said. "No, I don't. Oh, wait, yeah, vaguely. So what? You knew him?"

"No, I didn't know him. He just died, that's all. And I looked at your fingers and they were stubby and it made me see myself the way other people saw me, which was so unnerving, and then I sent you my English essay and then you never spoke to me again. It doesn't make any sense, Martha!"

Martha handed me a glass of water.

"Why didn't you just tell me you hated the story?"

"I'm sorry," Martha said.

I waited. At last. An explanation.

"I'm sorry, Jane, but I don't remember that drowning man very well, and I don't remember any story at all. Anyway, what's wrong with my fingers? I've always thought I had perfectly reasonable fingers."

She held them out to Gloria, who nodded approvingly.

"You hate my fingers?" Martha said. "How odd."

I awoke to a grinding, gnashing noise. I knew immediately that we had run aground. I lay in my bunk, still nauseated and dizzy, doped and weak, too frightened to move. The boat was not rocking. It actually seemed rather calm. Probably the water rushing in through the gigantic hole in the hull was stabilizing the doomed craft. I wondered how long we had. I felt the cold sweat on my forehead, on my chest, my arms. I wondered if it was fever or fear. My life jacket was on a shelf above me. If only I had the strength to stand up and put it on. Sleepiness battled with adrenaline and terror.

I forced my eyes open. "Gloria, we're, like, sinking."

"Do you think we ran aground? Or hit a reef or something? What a noise! I wonder if we've crossed the equator."

"I don't think it scrapes when you cross the equator. Anyway, we'll drown in either hemisphere."

We lay quietly for a while. I sweated and waited for the captain to make his announcement. Then I realized I had fallen back to sleep and I pulled myself to consciousness, embarrassed that on the verge of death I had taken a nap.

Then I said, "What if we sink?"

"But we seem to be moving," Gloria said.

"So? There's a huge hole in the boat! We'll go down in a whirlpool, like the *Pequod*. Have we crossed the equator or not? I won't even know what direction the whirlpool will swirl in."

There was a knock on the door. This was it. The captain telling us to abandon ship. Would they start to ring the little bell they used to summon us for meals? Where were the lifeboats? The engine still roared behind us.

Now I would die. My whole short life had been lived in a jumble of improperly catalogued perceptions, everything filed carefully in the wrong drawer, and now I would die, I would sink to the bottom of the sea having understood nothing.

The door opened. Martha poked her head inside.

Oh God, I thought. You've come personally to deliver the bad news. We really *are* sinking. I tried to console myself with the thought that we had reconciled before dying.

"Jane, are these yours?" Martha said.

In the light from the deck I could see some sort of cloth hanging from her hand.

"It looks like maybe a blue shirt, maybe a pair of those hiking shorts. Wasn't that what you had on this morning? Found them in the boat's main exhaust fan. What a racket. At first I thought we'd gone aground." She held them up, two carefully selected items of clothing perfect for an equatorial nature cruise, now tatters, shredded boisterously but efficiently by a ship's fan.

First I had polluted an island that an entire government spent a large proportion of its strained budget trying to protect from the introduction of foreign matter. Then, with my stained, guilty clothes, I had sabotaged a boat.

"Very Robinson Crusoe," Martha said, tossing the rags on the bed. As she turned to leave, I could see her through the dim cabin, in the doorway, against the dark, clear sky.

"Did we cross the equator yet?" Gloria called after her in a groggy voice.

—————

When the wake-up bell rang, I crawled out of bed and blinked in the morning light. In the dining room, the other passengers clapped and cheered at my recovery. I wore my last intact pair of nylon quick-drying many-pocketed shorts.

"Late last night, passengers aboard a familiar seagoing bark were startled by loud, violently scraping noises," said Jeremy Toll. "The hullabaloo lasted mere seconds and remains, as of the following morning, shrouded in mystery."

"No, no," Mr. Tommaso reassured me. "Martha said it was just something that got caught in the fan."

"Poor little endangered species," Mrs. Tommaso said. "Probably."

12

⁓⟋⟋⟋⟋⟋⟋⟋⟋⟋⟋⁓

W‍E SPENT the last full day of the trip on Santa Cruz, an island whose volcanic slopes display a range of vegetation that exactly follows the most emblematic of diagrams you see in books
about the Galapagos—bands of like-minded plants, from the saltbush of the littoral zone all the way up to the club moss of the
misty pampa zone. Santa Cruz, in its diversity, has a town, too, a
picturesque gathering of white one-story structures and half-built
boats perched in their scaffolding, called Puerto Ayorta. Depend-
ing on when in the last fifteen years our guidebooks had been pub-
lished, they informed us that the population of Santa Cruz was
anywhere from four thousand to twenty thousand.

"They've paved the roads," Jack said. "It looks so different."

"You never came here before," Dot said.

"I've seen pictures."

"Poser," said Dot.

"*Poseur*," Jeremy said gently.

As we walked through the town to the Darwin Research Center,

Jack made no other comments, no observations about flora or fauna or geological formations. He did not march up front beside Martha as he usually did. He no longer exhibited his knowledge for Martha's approval or correction. He did not smile or make jokes or offer me a drink from his water bottle. He walked in uncharacteristic silence, looking mild and distracted. He seemed, in fact—and it was almost inconceivable, so that it took me a while to come up with the right word—lost. Having accomplished his mission, he seemed less like the teacher's pet than the teacher's pet on summer vacation, purposeless, aimless, nothing to do for months and months. He also seemed, like a child with nothing to do for months and months, relieved.

Still a little weak, I brought up the rear of the procession.

"Are you okay?" Jack said.

"Everyone is so kind." I realized I sounded like Scarlett O'Hara. No, not Scarlett. Like what's-her-name, Ashley's wife, the simpering one.

"Are you okay?" Jack said to his mother.

"I'm bereft," his mother answered. "*If* you don't mind."

Poor Jack. His work was done. His father was scattered.

"A very goal-oriented young man," Gloria whispered, nodding at him. "Poor dear."

I felt sorry for Jack, too, now rudderless, as if he'd lost his faith.

"Look," I said, poking him the way Martha used to poke me. "A sesuvium."

Jack turned, fingered a leaf.

"It's a saltbush," he corrected me, without much enthusiasm. He tore off a leaf. "Taste it."

"Salty," I said.

He seemed cheered, just a little.

"Jane, are you okay today?" Martha asked me. "I was worried about you last night. You were sort of babbling incoherently."

Babbling incoherently. I had pondered the nature of friendship, had dissected and scrutinized it, had theorized and deduced its origins, had witnessed its extinction and excavated its fossilized remains, and the sum of this adventure in natural history was incoherent babbling.

"Oh, yeah," I said. "The sun, you know? Fine, I'm fine now."

The research center was a touching, deeply human place. I, of course, saw it as a metaphor for all of human endeavor. Martha, of course, objected strenuously to such an interpretation. But what else can you say about a place in which people devote their lives to breeding endangered tortoises other people have spent centuries endangering? Some of the tortoises were babies, the size of the pet turtles we used to have in school. They crawled around their shady nurseries, labeled by island and species. Then we went into the bigger corrals of the bigger tortoises. They stared at us. They stretched out their necks. They plodded toward us. They were huge. They were as grand as pianos.

A tortoise, its eyelids drooping over ancient, cloudy eyes, began chewing on one of Mrs. Tommaso's bright green trouser legs.

She said, "Shoo!"

There was a slide show in the visitors' center about the threat of feral dogs to baby iguanas and the threat of feral goats and donkeys to the vegetation the tortoises needed to survive. Mrs. Tommaso was visibly distressed by this presentation.

"The poor . . ." She stopped, unable to decide which species to worry about first—the iguanas? the dogs? and those sweet-looking donkeys!—stunned by cognitive dissonance as by an electric shock. "The poor . . ."

"Things," Gloria suggested.

We followed a boardwalk past more corrals until we found Lonesome George. He was the last of his kind, perhaps the only real individual in the world. There were no other Pinta tortoises left. The research center occasionally tried to stimulate him manually, as Martha delicately put it, in order to preserve some of his sperm. Just in case another Pinta turned up somewhere.

The idea that we would all return home the next day suddenly struck me, and struck me as very sad. *I* would be lonesome, like Lonesome George.

"Well, not exactly," Gloria said.

"The tortoises can live over a hundred years," Martha was saying. "What if a sailor in, say, 1881 took a tortoise home from Pinta to his wife? It might have lived as a pet all these years. It might yet be discovered and brought home to old George. Or to his sperm. His old sperm. Or so one hopes. They've tried mating George with other species. They could then mate him with his daughter, and then his granddaughter, and the strain would be almost pure again."

"A trifle Appalachian," Jeremy said.

"The last time I was here," Martha said, "we saw two tortoises mating. The shells provide a challenge. Luckily, the male has a forked penis."

Martha described the left penis, the right penis, and Lonesome George's unhappy attempts to use his own ambidextrous member, all to Dot's wide-eyed, snorting delight, then moved on to the different shapes of the shells of different species, by which they could be told apart and which allowed them to eat at different levels, some grazing like sheep, some reaching up into the trees like giraffes.

When Darwin came to the Galapagos, he rode on the backs of

tortoises. They live to be so old that it was even possible, or almost possible, which was good enough for me as I stood there surrounded by their enormous shells, that Darwin had ridden on the back of one of these very creatures. Darwin timed them as they lumbered to and from a watering hole. He was told by the governor of the Galapagos that one could identify which island a tortoise came from by the shape of its shell, but Darwin didn't realize the significance of that information until much later. I think the *Beagle* crew took a young tortoise with them on their journey and that it died, but I'm not sure. Maybe that was Melville. Martha told us that whalers used to load up on tortoises and store them upside down in the hold. Six months later, they could haul one out, still alive, and slaughter it for fresh meat and turtle soup.

"It's okay," Jeannie reassured Mrs. Tommaso, who again looked alarmed. "Sailors must be *practical* and keep up their *strength!*"

Martha led us through the research center and told us more stories. She had a story for everything. Turtle penises seemed as dramatic to her as volcanoes. Even the family feud had a story. Perhaps the feud was not as stirring as Lonesome George's sex life, but still Martha, the raconteur, had been able to unfold a tale of lovers, of broken engagements. Because she liked so much to narrate, to report and explain and instruct, it puzzled me once again that she had never offered her version of the end of our friendship. I had offered mine: incoherent babbling.

Perhaps friendship has no end, meaning no intent, no goal, and so no narrative structure. I wondered again what evolutionary value friendship could possibly hold. There are theories about cooperation, I know, but friendship is hardly that. I suppose it could be some remnant of parental love or sibling love or family love in general. That makes sense. Just a vestige, though, like the male nipple.

We walked on the recently paved road into the town, past the bright tourist boutiques. There were quite a few boats anchored in the harbor, and the town was busy and lively. I bought a T-shirt with iguanas on it.

Martha smiled at it, a little condescendingly, I thought.

"Well, I can always wear it to the gym."

Gloria bought a boobies T-shirt, which said "Boobies" across the chest.

"And *I* don't go to a gym," she said.

"So many new shops," Martha said. "When I'm away for a few weeks, another always springs up."

Martha, what are you doing here? I thought. I have been with you for seven days on this trip, cheek by jowl, and I still have no idea.

"This shop wasn't here two weeks ago," Martha said, walking into a boutique. We all followed her and began fingering the merchandise, beautiful dresses and jackets and bags made from some kind of tightly woven, brightly patterned Ecuadorian material.

"This is awfully chic for Puerto Ayorta," Martha said.

The stuff was surprisingly elegant, not at all like the usual tourist-bound native crafts. Gloria eyed it suspiciously.

"Where is this from?" she asked the man behind the counter.

"Wife," he said. He called in Spanish into a back room, and Wife stuck her head out. She looked at me. She looked at Martha. A cigarette hung from her mouth. A Winston.

"Son of a bitch!" she said.

"No, no, they're lovely," Gloria said. "I just wondered —"

"Son of a bitch!" Graziela said, holding out her arms, enfolding Martha and me in a hug.

The sound of Graziela's voice, the sound of Martha's laugh, and the smell of tobacco came together, a heady atmosphere of com-

fortable memory and confused, unlikely disorder. What was Graziela doing in the Galapagos? What are you doing here, Martha
had asked me at the beginning of the trip, and I had answered, My
mother sent me.

"Did my mother send you?" I asked Graziela.

Graziela offered me, then Martha, a cigarette.

Graziela gestured to the man behind the counter. "Husband,"
she said. Then she expanded the gesture to take in the whole store,
of which she was obviously equally fond. "Shop."

"Boutique," said Husband.

"Castro, kiss my ass!" Graziela said.

Her English, while still colorful, was not any better than it had
been ten years ago. Martha spoke to her in Spanish, though, and
ascertained that Graziela had been living in Guayaquil with her
husband, an Ecuadorian she'd met in the States. They had just expanded their business to Santa Cruz, opening the third of their
line of dress shops in that country.

Graziela picked out dresses for us. "No union label!" she said.

Her husband gave everyone discounts.

"Hamburger!" Graziela cried, and led all of us off to a restaurant.

Is this why I'm here? I thought. Did I come here to find you, to
find the past in this antediluvian place, to smoke cigarettes with
my antediluvian friends? Was Gloria wrong, after all, and had I
succeeded in digging up the old bones of friendship, in slapping
the skin and feathers back on like Darwin's ostrich rescued from
the stewpot?

Graziela and Martha chatted in Spanish. Graziela made sure to
turn to me and, in English, swear like a sailor as she petted my
cheeks and threw up her hands in astonished delight at the va-
garies of fortune that had brought us together again. Martha trans-

lated the most important parts. But we were not little girls in Barlow distracting the housekeeper from her duties. We were not best friends bumming cigarettes off Aunt Anna and her companion. Aunt Anna was dead, Graziela was a married entrepreneur, and Martha and I were distant cousins.

We took our farewell of Graziela, who gave me her card, which had a tiny green turtle in the upper-right-hand corner, and Martha guided us to a dusty blue bus. I waved to Graziela. She blew a kiss and called out, "Dirty goddamn bastards!" with a big sentimental smile and tears rolling down her cheeks.

The bus rattled up a gravel road through a fertile humid zone, much of which was still farmed and privately owned, to a fern forest at the top of the lopsided central mountain. Martha guided us along a narrow path, identifying the vines and branches that brushed our faces. I remembered walking through our meadow of tall wildflowers in Barlow. I remembered the day I met Martha.

We came out into an opening and faced two cavernous holes, calderas, enormous bowl-shaped valleys overgrown with plants, every single one of which, it seemed, Martha insisted we look at through our binoculars. The calderas were called Los Gemelos, the Twins.

We were all wearing rain jackets to protect us from the famous mists that were supposed to blanket the higher elevations during that season, but the sky was clear and it was hot. The names of the plants did not interest me anymore, now that our trip was almost done. I tried to look carefully, though, if only for Jack's sake, to encourage him, keep his chin up, revive the teacher's pet in him.

"I'm actually a little tired of examining little leaves," he said. "And yet I don't want to go home, I don't ever want to leave. Funny, the end of a trip, isn't it?"

Martha guided us to a field where we saw two huge tortoises

grazing. A little farther on, a corpulent sow and a line of piglets ran past. The light was fading. The field looked like the English countryside, open and lush, a tall tree here and there swaying above the stone walls. It was a familiar scene, from hundreds of books and movies, from Masterpiece Theatre. Why was it here?

We were all standing, marveling at the appearance of barnyard animals. We said how cute they were. We jostled one another trying to get pictures. Martha leaned against a tree and looked on in disgust.

"You have come three thousand miles to a new hemisphere to take pictures of pigs?" she said.

We continued to watch the mother pig and her enormous piglets, comfortably scratching themselves against a tall, introduced tree. It was a homey scene, if your home happened to be Sussex. The tortoises, two of them, rare and lumbering through the grass, looked out of place, fragile. The parable of the tortoise and the pig.

"My father had a pig's valve in his heart," Jack said.

His mother began to dab her eyes. Mrs. Tommaso stared at him in anti-vivisectionist angst.

"Nothing is where it should be," Dot said.

"You have fine instincts," Jeremy said, patting her head proudly.

"Look, extinction is the counterpart of evolution," Martha said. "Let's go. It's getting late." She tried to round us up. "Come on. They're just pigs."

But we stood transfixed in a meadow that looked as if it had posed for an illustration of Dr. Dolittle's Puddleby-on-the-Marsh. When one stands in an evening field and the sky fades in a glorious wash of scarlet, and the barnyard animals are grunting, and lush green grass rolls in every direction, gently, to the horizon, and the faint scent of damp earth rises as the sun sets, even the presence of two Galapagos tortoises cannot obstruct a rush of almost hackneyed emotion, of delicious melancholy, of homesickness, of the impossibility of complete happiness and, at the same time, the unending need for it.

"This is a Caspar David Friedrich moment," Jeremy said, his voice hushed, awed.

"I want to go home," Dot said.

I thought of Barlow. I could almost smell my mother's lilacs.

"Come on, off we go," Martha said. She poked me.

How did you get here, Martha? I thought. How did you end up at home in the Galapagos like these pigs?

Unable to move us, Martha took a deep breath, then assumed her instructive role. "Those pigs and those tortoises are actually related. One way you can see it is when you examine the mammalian inner-ear bones. They are derived from reptilian jaw elements."

Probably you came here on a whim, just like me, I thought. Although surely you came on your own whim, not your mother's. Fate, which is to say, whim, brought us together. And Fate, which is to say, whim, would separate us again.

"For the last hundred, hundred and fifty years, a lot of zoology has been the study of phylogeny, that is, tracing an organism's form back to a common ancestor, and so reconstructing that common ancestor. It's a limited way of looking at evolution, but it has yielded some interesting descriptions."

If a century of zoologists could devote their lives and their monographs to such a pursuit, surely I was within my rights attempting to trace friendship, this oddest of all organisms, back to its roots.

"When two organisms have attributes that derive from an equivalent characteristic of a common ancestor," Martha was saying, "they are said to be homologous."

Why weren't Martha and I homologous?

"Would you say you and I are homologous?" I asked Martha.

"Why? Because we both have Barlow in our name?" She laughed. "You're so literal-minded and fanciful at the same time."

I was, wasn't I? A black hole, sucking up the world around me to metaphorize it out of all recognizability. Darwin was right—the habit of comparison leads to generalization. He was right—we travelers stay such a short time, able to make mere sketches of what we've seen. And then we fill up the wide gaps of knowledge with inaccurate and superficial hypotheses.

Wasn't that what Martha did as well? No. Martha told stories, but she described what she saw. Detailed observation—just what Darwin valued. The world opened up before her, inspired by her vision and her touch. She used what she found, like my father opening all those misfiled drawers. Whereas all I seemed to do was put things in the drawers. I was the one who misfiled in the first place.

I wondered how much of my life I had misfiled over the years. Had I misfiled my ex-husband, Michael? Obviously. Although whether I had misfiled him under "Husband" or had misfiled him under "Ex-husband" was anybody's guess. Probably both. I had certainly misfiled Martha. And our friendship.

Let's pretend friendship is a species. One possibility is extinction. I had searched my memory for an event that precipitated the end of our friendship. A sudden change in climate, a meteor, a story of a drowned man. But our friendship was not extinct, for I still carried it with me. If a species has not become extinct, yet has not survived, it must have changed. Easy enough. The species had changed. Gloria had theorized that this change left Martha reduced to a remnant, an organ that had lost its usefulness and so shrunk and not quite disappeared. But I finally realized, as I stood and watched those pigs with their mammalian ear bones derived from reptilian jaw structures, that it was not Martha who was the residual organ.

Here is something I read in Darwin's journal. He was amused by a theory of a contemporary philosopher, William Whewell. "Says length of days [is] adapted to duration of sleep of man!!! & not man to planets," Darwin wrote. "Instance of arrogance!!"

I pulled Gloria aside. "I got it backward," I said. "Like Whewell."

"I'm sorry."

"The sun does not bend itself to man's needs. It's the duration of man's sleep that is the adaptation. Our sleep is the accommodation to the earth's rotation, to the cycle of the sun and the planets," I said. "That explains everything."

It was so obvious. I had—"instance of arrogance!!"—been looking at it upside down, backward. I had assumed that the length of the night was the result of my need for sleep. For years I had been asking myself what I could have done to Martha, an action of which I thought nothing at the time, but which cut her to the quick, something unforgivable, unforgivable even to Martha. I had come up with so many possible explanations. The note with the heart and the question mark. An inadvertent slight. My story about that poor drowned man.

But it had nothing to do with me or my story. It had to do with Martha, with her story, with her rotations, her travels from dawn to dusk, from horizon to horizon, whatever they were, whatever they had been, journeys beyond my sight that had nothing to do with me, the other side of the moon.

"You see, Martha is the sun —"

Gloria nodded in an indulgent, teacherly way.

"And *I'm* the male nipple."

There was no mystery to it. There was no forgiving or not forgiving. There was no meteor, no saltation.

"God, what a relief," I said.

The splitting event was, as splitting events are, a haphazard affair, an accident, a shift of direction that was, in hindsight, an opportunity, an occurrence with no meaning other than its ultimate but unintended outcome.

"I'm the whale's thumb. I was so arrogant and self-centered that I thought it must be Martha, but really it's *me! I'm* the vestigial organ."

I pointed at myself, poking myself in the chest.

"Me," I said. "Me, me!"

"For six days she labored in order to discover humility," Gloria said. "On the seventh day, she rested."

—·——

Darwin wrote in one of his notebooks, "No structure will last without it is adaptation to *whole* life of animal, and not if it be solely to the womb, as in monster, or solely to manhood—it will decrease and be driven outwards in the grand crush of population." That statement was in the fourth of the transmutation notebooks, which Darwin labeled "E," and which was written in gray or brown ink and bound in rust-brown leather with cream-colored labels and a broken clasp. I have not read the notebook bound in rust-brown leather. I read a paperback edition. But I like to imagine the book itself, the weight of it, the smell.

In the same notebook, Darwin hypothesized on the possible reason for the existence of the sexes. I mean, what are they here for? It would be so much simpler without them. But evolution needed sexes and sexual reproduction, thank God, so that natural selection could work on whole populations, rather than just individuals. "My theory," Darwin wrote, "gives great final cause (I do not wish to say only cause, but one great final cause—nothing probably exists for one cause) of sexes in separate animals: for otherwise there be as many species as individuals." I read this line, several times, and understood it at last and was impressed by its astute, exuberant, imaginative simplicity, but what really struck me about this important passage was the insignificant aside "nothing probably exists for one cause."

Martha was very civil when I left and even asked for my address. Gloria gave me a pair of earrings as a keepsake, which may or may not have been fashioned from pigeon excrement.

The first night back in New York, Jack e-mailed me an article about species from *Scientific American*, a funny note, and an invitation to take-out Chinese at his 2B or mine. "Or is it not 2B?" To which I replied, "2B continued," and went home for the weekend to see my parents in Barlow.

"Did you get far enough away?" my father asked.

"Did you know that we don't really see objects, just the light reflected from them?"

"That's pretty far, I guess."

My mother stared at us.

"We should have sent you to Paris," she said.

"Did you have fun with Martha? What a small world it is," my father said. "Did you make lots of new friends, too?"

"Yes, actually. I did."

I took a walk past the Not Our Barlows', but no one was home.

"You didn't tell me you used to be engaged to Martha's father," I said to my mother.

"No, I didn't."

"I'm glad you didn't marry him," I said.

"Well, I couldn't, could I? I mean we *are* brother and sister."

My father offered me a Scotch.

I drank the Scotch and waited for my mother to say something like, "Metaphorically speaking, of course, ha ha!" But she didn't. She said, "You always wanted a love child in the family. Now you've got one. Robert Barlow."

"He's not a Barlow?"

"Oh, he's a Barlow all right," my father said.

"Your grandfather Edwin, my father, was once engaged to the suffragette. She left Edwin for Hamilton Barlow, who was Edwin's first cousin."

I ran through the names in my head. Hamilton was Franklin's son. Hamilton was Martha's grandfather, and the suffragette who married him instead of my grandfather was Martha's grandmother.

"Hamilton was older than my father," my mother was saying. "Hamilton was richer."

"They'd already screwed your grandfather," my father said. "Hamilton and Franklin sold assets without his approval, hid profits. Your grandpa Edwin and aunt Anna were left almost penniless. I've told you about that. Well, Anna had her house. Edwin had this house. But the Not Our Barlows got the dough."

So the suffragette dumped Edwin, that handsome man in the white suit in the photographs from Cuba. She left him for Hamilton, the rich cousin with the mustache. I'd seen pictures of Hamilton, too, thumbs tucked in his waistcoat pockets. Hamilton and the suffragette got married. And Edwin got a job in Cuba and married the boss's daughter.

Did Martha know this? Did she want to know it? Perhaps I would write to her and tell her someday.

"My uncle Hamilton and aunt Suffragette had a son," my mother said. "That was Robert. But . . . Uncle Hamilton was not Robert's father. Uncle Hamilton was Robert's uncle."

"Huh?"

"The suffragette really was progressive, I suppose. At any rate, she was already pregnant when she married Hamilton. My *father* was Robert's father."

"That makes Robert your *brother*," I said. "You can't be engaged to your brother!"

"My feelings exactly. My father had to go to Cuba, start over. He met my mother, got married, had me. Robert and I met at a college mixer. Isn't that absurd? We realized we were cousins from feuding sides of the same family. It was all very Romeo and Juliet. Until he told his mother we were getting engaged and she told him who his real father was. Then it was a bit Siegmund and Sieglinde."

"That's disgusting," I said.

"True," said my father.

"*Operatic*," said my mother.

"I prefer to think that your mother was too seasick to marry old Robert Barlow."

"Well, that, too," my mother said. "I don't think my father ever knew. Thank God. Aunt Anna did. And, really, that suffragette jezebel person could have changed the sheets."

"Indeed," said my father. "A feud is a many-splendored thing."

"Did you have clean sheets on your boat, Jane? I hope Martha was well. My niece. What an odd place for her to end up. Well, she always liked scampering around the woods. Pleasant little girl, all things considered. You know, Brother Robert and his new wife are thinking of opening that wretched bed and breakfast again. Why don't they open it in the Galapagos? Thank God Graziela got her shop. *Querido*, should we go to visit her? Martha can be our guide. Show us your pictures, Jane, dear. Daddy and I want to go to the Galapagos Islands. Perhaps I can get a cutting of some darling wildflower."

"Yes, show us the sheep photos, Jane."

"No sheep," I said. "Pigs."

They came out beautifully, the sun setting in a bright pink sky, the shadows of the trees, the green turf.

My mother looked at the photograph of the pigs with a tender smile.

"Chaos," she said.